A DEAL GONE WRONG

A Carlos Alvarado Mystery Book One

A Carlos Alvarado Mystery

In reading order:

A Deal Gone Wrong

The Fair Park Slasher

(Coming: 2026)

A DEAL GONE WRONG

A Carlos Alvarado Mystery Book One

SAUL SANDOVAL

WICKED INK

PUBLISHING

A Deal Gone Wrong (A Carlos Alvarado Mystery) : Book 1
Copyright © 2025 by Saul Sandoval

Published by Wicked Ink Publishing Ltd.
www.wickedinkpublishing.com

Cover and book design © 2025 by Wicked Ink Publishing Ltd.
Editors: Raymond Griffiths & Adam Bamford

First Edition: May 2025
Printed in Canada

A Deal Gone Wrong / Saul Sandoval. — Calgary, Alberta : Wicked Ink Publishing Ltd., 2025.
ISBN 978-1-998278-13-8 (paperback)
ISBN 978-1-998278-14-5 (ebook)
1. Mystery fiction. 2. Detective and mystery stories. 3. Rio Grande Valley—Fiction. 4. Detective fiction series. I. Title.
Book 1 of the A Carlos Alvarado Mystery series.
Text in English. Audience: General Adult
This is a publisher-supplied cataloguing record.

Para mi padre. (For my dad).

A DEAL
GONE WRONG

A Carlos Alvarado Mystery Book One

The glimmer of second chances might just prove to be deadly...

1

After all these years, Detective Carlos Alvarado would still sometimes get a phantom smell of his sister's rose oil perfume in the brisk wind of the warm summer's night.

Parked on Rangerville Road on the west side of Valley City, Carlos sat quietly in his unmarked Ford Explorer, writing in his notebook. It was after midnight and pedestrian traffic was light to nonexistent.

As he wrote, he kept one eye on the corner apartment. Even though no cars had passed in the last several hours, Carlos maintained his vigilance. He had gotten wind from "Reggie", one of his confidential informants that Roger Martinez, a local speed dealer, would be around sometime tonight. From his glove box, Carlos pulled a container of caffeine pills and popped a couple. He wanted to be sharp if Roger showed up. He fumbled around searching for his cigarettes but remembered he smoked his last one that morning. Lucky for him, he always left an "emergency" cigarette under his visor.

He grabbed the cigarette from under the visor elastic band

where the picture of his younger sister, Amanda, glided onto his lap. She would have been twenty-four this year if it hadn't been for The Fair Park Slasher. Immediately following her death, the police did their best but could not find the killer. In fact, the killer went silent. The police couldn't draw a link between both events, but Carlos always felt something was off.

Carlos glanced toward the apartment buildings, all of them the same. Each was five stories tall, with rows of windows and an old-school fire escape on its side. The sand-coloured brick looked pale next to the waving palm trees that lined the street.

There was only one streetlamp per two buildings and many dark spots on the street, which Roger surely took advantage of. Without warning, a light in the second-floor row came on.

Carlos grabbed his Glock 22 from under the seat and latched on his bullet-proof vest before exiting. He crept along the sidewalk in the shadows, his gun in hand, pointed down.

As Carlos approached Roger's building, a dark figure passed the second story middle window. Carlos made his way up the fire escape stairs leading to the window. Tiptoeing up the steps, he threw the safety off his gun and crouched a few steps below the window. Through a crack in the mini blinds, he caught a glimpse of Roger. He was sitting down at a makeshift poker table. Since Roger had his back turned, Carlos was unable to see what he was doing. A knock came from his door, and Roger went to answer it.

On the table, Carlos saw clear baggies of a white crystalline rock, likely speed, divided up for sale. Along with it, a lockbox with other loose rocks was open. Seeing the potential drugs and his setup for sales and distribution, Carlos had what he needed and made his way back down the steps. Carlos' heart raced with a mixture of trepidation and anticipation. Almost every time he had Roger on the ropes, something always went wrong. This time, he had all his ducks in a row and would get it right.

At the base of the fire escape, he took a moment to calm his breathing down, having not noticed that he was breathing rapidly increased in all the excitement. Dead ends always came up regarding the Fair Park Slasher case, but it didn't stop him from tracking down every lead, no matter how insignificant. With his mind clear and his breathing under control, he was ready.

Around the corner, he entered the building, careful to avoid making any unnecessary noise, and made his way up the stairwell to Roger's floor. Inside the stairwell, a foul whiff of bleach and dirty mop hit Carlos' nose, causing him to almost lose his balance as he tiptoed his way up and using his long-sleeved shirt to handle the rails, hoping to reduce his noise level further.

Before Carlos opened the hallway door, it opened toward him. A tweaker in a hoodie popped out and froze, glancing down at Carlos' gun and bolted past him down the stairs. Carlos ignored him and entered the hallway. Inside, every fourth light worked and flickered as if the power might go out at any moment.

The numbers were hardly visible, but Carlos knew Roger's was the third on the left since it faced the street side. When he arrived at the apartment, he placed his ear to the door just out of the peephole view and heard some shuffling. He then heard what sounded like a butane torch cracking on a few times.

Thump! Thump! Thump!

"Valley City PD, Detective Alvarado. Open up," Carlos said. There was silence, and then a loud crash.

"Open the door now," yelled Carlos.

Still no response. Carlos took a step back and kicked the door in. The frame came apart, and the door flew open with wood particles scenting the air with saw dust like pieces. Inside, he found the poker table on the ground, along with the bags of clear, smoky, chunky crystals what Carlos deduced must be speed.

The room was quiet but gave off a distinct odour of burning plastic, but it seemed to fade when Carlos recognized the smoke residue from smoking speed. Carlos pointed his gun in the room and slowly made his way in, tapping the bathroom door open, but found no one. The bathroom lights flickered, and the toilet bowl tank slowly dripped as it filled.

Bang!

Carlos turned just in time to see the window shut and Roger fleeing down the fire escape.

"Police! Stop!"

Carlos continued down the steps anyway and fired a shot past Roger through the window as a warning. The raw acrid odour of gunpowder wafted up Carlos' nose, burning his nostrils. The window in the foreground shattered and the debris just missed Roger, who didn't even pause. Carlos then opened the other window and pursued him down the steps.

Once outside and downstairs, Carlos made his way around the building and down the street where he had parked, firing another shot in the air, hoping to scare Roger, who stopped in his tracks next to a dumpster where he put his hands up. Carlos made his approach slowly and stopped a couple of feet short. He had to get his breathing under control to avoid hyperventilating, so he took three long breaths before speaking.

"Turn around. I have two questions for you."

Roger turned around and wore a smile the size of a Cheshire cat.

"I'm not gonna answer any," said Roger, interrupted by Carlos' gun at his temple.

"You were saying shit face," Carlos said, as he redirected his aim toward Roger's crotch.

"Like I was saying, I have two questions. Number one. Who's your supplier, and number two? What do you know about the Fair Park Slasher? Answer me."

"Fuck you talking about? I ain't giving my source up. You're stupid, and I never heard of no fair park slasher." Roger even made his smile bigger.

Carlos' heart raced and his chest tightened. His anger rose from the depths of his stomach. The only thing he hated more than drug dealers were liars.

"Fair Park Slasher! What do you know? Tell me, fucker." Carlos' face beaded sweat, and his eyes twitched. He applied pressure with the gun even further.

"I know nothing about the Fair Park Slasher. I don't even know what that is. And you know I can't give up my source. It's not happening." Roger winked at Carlos.

Before Carlos spoke, a two-by-four board whacked him across the head and dropped him to his knees. Someone was hiding behind the dumpster and caught him off guard. His hands weakened as he tried to point the gun back at Roger. The hidden assailant easily kicked it out of his hands. There was that smile again before everything went black with the force of another whack on his head.

He regained consciousness minutes later.

"Detective, you all right?" asked Sergeant Moody.

"One neighbour heard the gunshots and called 911. We found you here next to the dumpster, bleeding from your head."

"I was on a stakeout waiting for the perp to get home. I pursued him out of his apartment when I got hit from behind.

That's all I remember. Did you find anything in the apartment upstairs? Did you find the drugs?"

"Detective, we did a thorough sweep of the apartment and found nothing strange. There was some furniture turned over, but that's about all. By the way, Captain Rankin wants to see when you're done here."

"Tell the captain I'm not feeling well. My head is killing me. Will you?" Carlos asked.

"He wants to know what you were doing here and why you busted into his apartment without calling for backup. But maybe you should go to the ER first."

"Look, I'm not feeling so hot. You tell him I'll drop by the hospital, but I'm going home right after, ok?" Carlos then made his way toward his Explorer.

"Detective, I'm sorry, but the captain gave me strict orders that if you weren't feeling good that someone should drive you to the hospital. Let Officer Thomas here take you and we'll drop off your truck at the hospital for you, ok?"

"Fine, but I don't have to like it. Don't mess up my truck, Moody!"

"Yes, sir," said Moody, shaking his head.

Inside Thomas' patrol vehicle, he grabbed a cigarette from his pocket and glanced at his sister's photo that he had tucked away in wallet one more time. He made a promise to himself that he would find out what happened to her. Tomorrow he would begin again. The flashing lights faded into the darkness in the rearview mirror as they sped toward Valley Baptist Medical Center for a quick checkup, then hopefully home to sleep it off.

THE NEXT MORNING, CARLOS SAT AT HIS DESK IN the corner near the window and finished typing his report on the Martinez case from last night. Outside, he glanced across the street onto the open field that is sometimes used as a soccer field but today was empty, much like how Carlos felt.

As he looked across the room, he had the best vantage point. Rotating detectives and other officers used the room from time to time, which had several rows of desks. The rows were bisected in the middle, creating a makeshift pathway that led to the captain's office, which stood at the top of a reverse sunken floor plan, which meant everyone in the office would have to look up to him. It was a strange design that Carlos never much liked.

His office also had all glass surrounding windows, each with privacy blinds. There was no mistake. When he made detective almost eight years ago, he made sure that his captain placed him in the corner. He wanted to see everyone at the same time. He didn't want any surprises. From his seat, he could see Captain Rankin's office. He tried not to look toward him because he had yet to finish his report on what happened last night.

The captain was on the phone with someone. His office door and blinds were open, thus giving everyone a glimpse into his office. His hands were stomping on his desk, causing the pictures of his kids to flop back and forth. He was screaming now, and his muffled conversation was full-on theatre for everyone in the detective's section to hear. As the conversation grew quieter, the captain seemed to gravitate towards his Ironman stress ball that had seen better days. The captain unexpectedly jumped up, but his knees collided with his desk, creating a loud crash that couldn't go unnoticed.

He dropped the phone and headed for his office door, stepping down two steps in obvious pain and annoyance yelling.

"ALVARADO!"

Rankin made a circling hand gesture rapidly.

"Captain?"

Carlos stood up and looked at Rankin, but did not move.

"Stop staring at me and get your ass over here."

Rankin snapped his fingers.

Carlos moved past Detective Johnson's desk, who was off duty, and Detective Salinas' desk. Salinas was quietly reading something on his computer and taking notes. Carlos entered Rankin's office.

"Sit," ordered Rankin.

Carlos casually sat in the chair and slumped, sinking down into its plush cushions. He glanced around the small office, every spare space on the wall covered with some medal or award or diploma. Rankin had crumpled up packs of Pall Malls in his trash, even though smoking wasn't allowed in the building. The air smelled of Ozium and coffee.

"Nice La-Z-Boy, Capt."

"Stop pretending that nothing shitty happened last night, like you didn't go on a stakeout without backup, not informing anyone, and, not to mention, discharging your weapon multiple times and, oh, my favourite, getting knocked unconscious by a drug dealer. Is that it? Did I miss anything?"

Captain always had a tendency to overreact to everything, and Carlos had learned to give him a wide berth for his unique way of leadership. What Carlos never got over was how awful the combination of spent cigarettes and burnt breath made more close quarters conversation and Rankin was one to always lean in and close talk to you. In fact, sometimes he would be so close that Carlos could pick out the grey hairs in his facial hair and receding hairline. It was not something he enjoyed doing but a grin and bear moment that would soon pass as long as Carlos smiled and nodded. Because of his position, Rankin wore a suit more times than not, and today was no exception. His dark grey suit made his pale face even paler and almost Casper like. The thin eyebrows didn't help either.

"Don't overstate things, Captain. Martinez has been on my radar for a while now, and last night as I was heading home, one of my confidential informants tipped me he would be home, so I went and waited. The 'shitty' thing that happened, Captain, was that somehow one of his accomplices —that I had no clue was there—cleaned up the place, leaving no fucking evidence other than my word."

"Exactly. Your word. I have got to ask, how many drug dealers have you busted in the last six months alone?"

"I don't know. Two or three. Why?"

"Why are you wasting your time with such low-level bullshit? You're better than that, Alvarado."

"Those fuckers deserve to be off the street."

"That may be so, but I have something else for you. I got a fresh case. Do you remember Coach Morelo from our softball league?" Rankin stood up from his chair and closed the blinds in his office, including the ones on his door, and tenderly shut it.

"Of course."

"When his neighbour found him, he was dead in his house, slumped over his kitchen table. His coffee and toast were still in front of him when his neighbour found him."

Back at his desk, Rankin scrolled his mouse down a couple of pages on his computer.

"Mrs. Fuentes is her name. Apparently, Coach Morelo would sometimes help her with her yard work and had come over to ask if he was free. She knocked several times and got no response. Making her way to the backyard, she went through the side gate and knocked on the back patio door. She found it open, let herself in, and found Coach Morelo at his kitchen table, unresponsive. She called 911. That's all we have for now. There's a unit on the scene, and they are expecting you."

Rankin shook his head twice.

"Find out what happened. Start with the neighbour and keep me updated. Got it? And please get your shit together. This is important."

"They are all important, Captain."

Carlos left the office and grabbed his things from his desk before heading toward his next assignment. The name Morelo kept bouncing around his head. It wasn't an uncommon name, but not one he ran into that often.

The last Morelo he knew was his ex-boyfriend from high school. Carlos didn't enjoy leaving a case unfinished, but Rankin needed him to focus on the Morelo case instead. He would have to check up on Martinez when he had the time.

2

He was back on the west side of town, this time at the corner of Basin and Wichita near the Boys and Girls Club. He got up late and didn't have time to make his double espresso in the morning, so instead he stopped at Starbucks for an iced shaken espresso with three shots did the trick.

Carlos, who dressed less formally than most detectives, wore what he wore on any given day, a pair of dark wash athletic fit jeans, a solid colour tee shirt and some sort of light jacket to conceal his weapon. The darkness of his clothes did little to offset the brownness of his skin.

From what his father told him, there was some Native American blood in him, the Karankawa tribe, if he remembered correctly. Carlos figured that's where he inherited his dark-skinned tone and minor tracking skills from. His hair was usually short and cut close with a clipper. Most times it grew fast, which kept going to Sport Clips monthly to keep his dark wavy hair in check.

The sun in his eyes caused him to squint, making his

brown eyes turn a shade of hazel as he surveyed the area of Fair Park. Unless there was a connected case, he had little reason to visit the west side. Mostly, it was a quiet part of town and the only action this area got was the yearly Riofest when corn in the cups and Tejano music reigned supreme for a week.

As he drove down the long stretch of Wichita Street and approached Basin Street, it looked familiar. As he approached the house where Sergeant Moody waited, the house on the corner caught his eye. It was a bright yellow house with its porch cracked in half. The weeds had grown to the height of the now broken fence. Carlos had been here before. The cobwebs were clearing. He recognized the area, and it was all coming into place for him.

Arriving at the scene, Carlos exited his black Ford Explorer. Outside, he found it a lot quieter than he had expected. In fact, there was no one outside other than Sergeant Moody and Mrs. Fuentes.

Morelo neatly cut his lawn, and he adorned the sidewalk that led to the front door with two huge pine bushes. The house had a pale-blue paint job. A chain-link fence that was about shoulder height surrounded the front yard. Carlos approached Sergeant Moody and retrieved his black leather Valley City PD issued pocket notebook and his favourite Paper-mate Flair pen.

"What we got?"

Carlos scanned the house.

Moody's eyes seemed to narrow before speaking.

"Detective, I arrived on the scene at approximately nineteen forty-five hours in response to a 911 call from Mrs. Fuentes here. She approached the front entrance and knocked several times, and when there was no response, she went around the side of the house to the back porch entrance."

"Sergeant Moody, before you get too deep into it, I'm

gonna go look inside and see what I can find. Will you finish taking Ms. Fuente's statement?"

Carlos couldn't help and look at Sergeant Moody and find the guy strange. Not that he was abnormally tall, standing at six foot three, nor that he was already balding at only his mid-thirties, but what struck Carlos strange was the unkemptness and size of his beard and facial hair. It seemed to grow in every which direction and just seemed unprofessional. The rest of his uniform was tidy and in tiptop shape, so it made no sense to Carlos why Moody couldn't keep his personal grooming in check. The darkness of his facial hair against the whiteness of his skin made it all stand out the more. Carlos made mention to Rankin several times, but nothing came of it. It was more annoying than anything else.

"Of course, Detective."

Carlos advanced on the quiet home and made a mental note to get the rest of Ms. Fuente's statement from Moody after he finished checking out the house. Moody always had a way to summarize statements in an efficient manner, plus Carlos's speed reading had come a long way since the academy. Most of the lights were off.

He placed his notepad and pen in his pocket and retrieved some black nitrile gloves, which he quickly put on. He approached the home toward the side gate, which was already open. There was a side window, but the drapes prevented anyone from seeing anything inside.

As he entered the backyard, he retrieved his flashlight, as the bright golden sun had set and cast a slow-moving shadow that danced across the emerald lawn.

Carlos flicked the lights on to get a better view and entered the back dining room, where he found Mr. Morelo. A strange smell hit Carlos straight in the face. It seemed to be a mixture of incense and Old Spice aftershave.

The EMS who tried to revive Mr. Morelo, whose food was still on the table, left the kitchen table mostly untouched. A bowl of oatmeal and coffee was next to a copy of the *Valley Morning Star* opened to the sports section.

The adjacent room had once been a bedroom, but it transformed into an office. Inside was a small twin bed and two desks in an L shape, cornering the far side of the room. Carlos turned on the lights and found stacks and stacks of old newspapers, then checked the windows for signs of intrusion, but they remained locked and untouched. He moved on to the kitchen.

The kitchen was in a U-shaped setup. The coffee maker was on. There wasn't much else left on the counters. It seemed like no one had updated the kitchen in decades. Various shades of brown and beige dominated the cabinets and flooring. The linoleum checkered floor squeaked as Carlos' boots crossed the length of it. He peered inside every cabinet but found nothing out of the ordinary. The refrigerator was old and bare, though inside the freezer was one bottle of Makers Mark Whiskey, unopened.

Carlos went to the living room and found the keys to the truck outside, hanging from a hook near the front entrance. The worn-out Chevy outside also seemed undisturbed and carried what looked like a layer of thick dust and fallen dried leaves from the many trees from the nearby canals for some time. Carlos noticed that the living room was suspiciously empty of family photos or of anything that would make this house a home. There seemed to be two more rooms at the rear of the house.

Inside the first room, he found a large king-sized bed along with a dresser and a vanity mirror. No TV. Black light-blocking blinds covered both windows. Clothes and boxes that smelled of mothballs and looked hardly touched filled the closet to the brim. Nothing out of place in the dresser drawers.

There was a small business card at the edge of the mirror with the name Treasure Hills Graphics, Ruben Delgado, and some contact information. He took a quick picture of it with his phone and moved on to not disturb the scene further.

Carlos bent down to see the base of the bed, which seemed to have a solid wooden base that was wrapped around the entire bed. He started from one end of the bed to the other and tapped his knuckle on it to see what sounds came from it. It all sounded the same. A deep, grounded sound emanated each time. He kept tapping till he came to the end of the frame, where the sound changed to a higher pitch sound. He moved the bedding off the side and pushed off the mattress and box spring to the floor.

Carlos could now get a better glimpse of the base and found that part of the edge had chipped away from where it was grabbed. He reached into his pocket and grabbed his knife. He wedged it into the crack and popped open the wooden panel. Inside was a black metal cash drawer that gleamed with the light from his flashlight. He retrieved it, placed it on the bed, and found stacks of hundred-dollar bills mixed with other smaller bills.

Under all the bills was an old school vinyl bound ledger accounting book for the money in the box. It was larger than the cash box and seemed to be written in some sort of code. The only thing that made any sense were the dollar amounts. The book contained handwritten entries, and the pages disappeared almost with their delicate, almost see-through beige paper.

Carlos stopped for a moment and flipped the lights to the room on. He took photos with his phone of everything, including and especially the ledger.

After he finished, he put it back under the bed and left the panel open for it to be marked into evidence. Using the strongest setting of his light, he continued to search for other clues. The hairs on his hands and arms inched their way up. His neck tingled. Something was off.

The next room was all but empty except for another small twin bed and a dresser with all the pictures that had been missing from the living room. Pictures of Mr. Morelo and presumably his wife and his kids.

One picture stood out to Carlos, and he picked it up. It was a picture of a young man in his high school graduating cap and gown. The picture had a label that read 'Class of 2009, Valley High School, Henry Morelo.'

Carlos paused for a moment and popped his knuckles one by one. He continued to stare at the picture and wondered how he didn't notice the name Morelo before and made the connection, but now he knew for sure. The street name, the yellow house on the corner, it all came back to him.

Henry became a distant part of Carlos's memory until his graduation picture brought it all to the forefront. Flashes of Henry ran through his mind, and a deep pang entered his stomach. His insides twisted and turned and made him feel nauseous. He regretted having those iced espressos earlier without food.

He placed the picture back down on the dresser and edged it back in place, but when he did, another smaller piece of card-stock fell on the dresser. One side had a picture of a knife dripping blood in red and white shading, and the other had two lines of text: *"Looks like you were too late again, Detective Alvarado. Wanna play?"*

Without thinking, Carlos dropped his flashlight and stumbled back, tripping on the nightstand, causing him to fall back onto the twin bed. He stared at the words.

Was it true?

The beads of sweat trickled down his brow and into his lips. The bitter taste jolted him back to reality.

Was this a coincidence? Years of unfulfilled hatred rushed back. He closed his eyes and slowed his breathing. He wasted no time.

If he was to solve Mr. Morelo's death and find a link to the Fair Park Slasher, he needed to get going. *But what about Henry?*

3

Upon answering the call, Henry felt surprised to hear Detective Salinas on the other end and not someone from the funeral home.

He was sitting in his dorm room doing some homework. The voice that answered caught him off guard as it grumbled more than sounded normal. Henry's total disposition changed and almost knocked him back from his chair onto to back of his loft bed.

Henry wore a backward UNT cap and whatever clean shirt he could find nothing to say for shorts. Living in north Texas, his Mexican heritage was easy to spot and sometimes brought him trouble in school of primarily white individuals. His skin colour was lighter than most and often would go unnoticed, but whenever he spoke, his accent, he swore he couldn't hear, was a dead giveaway. Detective Salinas' gruff voice and thick accent was even thicker than his.

"Mr. Morelo, this is Detective Salinas from the Valley City Police Department. I'm calling about your father."

"Is there something wrong?"

"There is no easy way to say this, but your father died two nights ago."

Henry stayed silent for a moment. He didn't speak to his father in almost ten years, and his death caught him off guard. Henry didn't know how to react. He tried to push some feelings out, but nothing came. He wasn't sure what it meant.

"Wait, why are you calling me and not the funeral home? Did something else happen?"

There was a long pause on the detective's part.

"Your father's system contained small amounts of brodifacoum, also known as rat poison. The preliminary autopsy showed he was ingesting it for quite some time, likely for the last few weeks. We will tell more with further tests. He paid a visit to his primary care physician last week and reported experiencing bloody urine and diarrhea, which is a symptom of brodifacoum poisoning. Although there was no way to know that he was ingesting it for weeks. The doctor diagnosed it as a urinary tract infection and gave him some antibiotics to manage it."

His numbness turned to confusion and anger.

"Somebody poisoned my father," said Henry, as his voice cracked.

"We don't want to jump to conclusions. Unfortunately, we don't have much else to tell you now. We are doing a full investigation and, for now, considering this a homicide investigation. Until we have more information, we can't rule anything out. I promise, Mr. Morleo, we will find out what happened. Your father was a friend to the department."

Walking over to the window after closing his laptop, Henry looked out to Rodgers Quadrangle, where people were playing Frisbee Golf, sitting on his bed, continuing to peer out. "Really, you knew my father. How?"

"He coached our softball charity team every summer and made his beans every year for the Valley City Police Night Out event. The money he made on selling his beans, he'd donate back to us. Like I said, he was a friend of the department. So, believe me when I tell you we will find out what happened. We have assigned Detective Alvarado to his case. He will reach out to you soon, but feel free to reach him here anytime. Our department has a great relationship with the New Today Counselling Services. If you are interested, I can have Detective Alvarado provide you with their number as well. Again, I am sorry for your loss."

Just like that, his father's death turned into a murder, but who in the world would want to harm his father? Henry thought. He wondered how he was ingesting poison for so long without even knowing it. He needed to contact Detective Alvarado and discover what took place.

EVERY SUNDAY MORNING FOR BREAKFAST, IT WOULD be the same thing: fried eggs with refried beans and a tortilla. Of course, his mother had made the beans earlier in the morning and she freshly smashed them with lard, which gave the beans a shimmer.

Henry remembered eating the beans but never had watched his father make them, so they would almost be impossible to recreate. Henry's grumbling stomach brought him back to reality, realizing he hadn't eaten since he got the news of his father's death.

Henry Morelo stood in his father's kitchen, staring at a pot of water, not knowing where to begin. He had all the ingredients needed—at least he thought he did—laid out on the kitchen counter. Every time he tried in the past to cook his father's *frijoles charro*, they always came out hard and bland. Henry tried to remember the times he spent with his father watching him cook, but all he could remember was the aroma of beans boiling, bacon, and a dark, almost smoky cumin scent wafting throughout the house. In fact, that smell would be his alarm clock on Sunday mornings.

Making the trip down from north Texas in just under ten hours and arriving at an empty home made Henry feel uneasy. His mom died several years earlier of cancer, and his father lived alone in his childhood home.

It was a strange thing to arrive *home* and find it empty. Henry's father died so suddenly that all his things were still lying around, including his shoes which were still at the door, his coffee cup still filled with now cold decaf coffee, and the keys to his white Chevy still hung by the door.

Henry opened the refrigerator door and found it quite empty except for a Tupperware container filled to the brim; opening it, to his surprise, he found his father's beans. His father must have made them a few days before. The simple fact he held the last thing his father had ever made caused Henry to tear up. Looking over to the kitchen table, Henry could imagine his father sitting there on Sunday mornings, drinking his coffee, eating some hot beans, and reading the newspaper.

It was all too much, so he warmed up some beans and made himself a cup of coffee and sat down at the kitchen table in the same spot where his father used to, imagining how his father must have felt sitting there alone every day.

Both Henry's siblings lived out of state and never came to visit, and Henry hadn't talked to his father in over ten years. Coming home to his empty house, he regrets that now. A round dish holding change and tiny folded pieces of stapled paper were in the middle of the kitchen table. There were dozens of folded papers and a black flip notebook with lines after lines of scribbled numbers and dates.

Henry opened one of the folder papers and read 24-12. Every single paper had something similar. Just under the bowl sat last Sunday's sports section of the *Valley Morning Star*, the local newspaper. On the list of the week's games, he found several of them circled along with the dates. Henry matched those with the listings in the notebook.

It all made sense.

His father would always be on the phone on Friday nights, especially when a football game was on. Somebody named Ricky or Jose would come knocking on the door, wanting to buy a ticket for the game. Henry's father would run bets on who would win the game and by how much.

By selling a certain number of tickets every week, he had a system in place that guaranteed him at least a couple hundred in profits. It puzzled Henry because someone would use rat poison to kill a man over a few hundred dollars, especially considering he had a betting pool in place.

Something didn't add up to Henry. But what could it be?

4

Santos Morelo's Fridays always started the same, especially during the football season. Even after being retired for fifteen years, he would still wake up at 6:30.

At sixty-five years old, he was used to waking up at that hour. Santos would walk over to the kitchen, still in the dark, turn on his coffee maker, and start the brew. Almost immediately, golden nutty and caramelized scents wafted in the air. He then grabbed a bowl and filled it with an instant oatmeal packet that he pulled from the cupboard. Santos added a dash of cinnamon and two packets of sweet n' low and placed them in the microwave.

While he waited for it to cook, he would head outside for his copy of the *Valley Morning Star*. It was still muggy outside. The air carried an odd mixture of cut grass and fishy water coming from the algae laden lapping canal. It gave the newspaper a bitter, almost musty odour.

Tiny pockets of fog bordered his lawn, almost like a barrier keeping him from the outside world. He stopped for a minute to observe the sun peeking out from a cloud on the other side of the nearby canal, reminding him of his mornings growing up on his father's farm just outside of town. The sound of the quiet was something he could never forget, and even now, he missed that silence.

Dogs barked in the distance, sprinklers activated, and the neighbour's cat meowed for attention. The newspaper was damp from the morning mist and was almost too wet to handle, but he picked it up, anyway. Inside, he opened the newspaper in sections and spread them out on the kitchen table so they could dry out in time for his breakfast.

When his oatmeal was ready, he sat at his kitchen table like he did every morning. He added two scoops of creamer to his coffee, then grabbed the sports section and looked up local high school football games scheduled that night but noticing that his creamer needing refilling, so headed back to the kitchen cabinet.

Inside, behind the pink and white sugar packets, grabbed the creamer container but not before spotting the rat poison hiding in the back. He didn't recall placing it there, but left it where it was. Going back to the table, he pulled out his pocket notebook and scribbled in it, "Lakeview Tigers, Treasure Hills Pirates, and Riverview Spartans."

He placed his half-eaten oatmeal off the side and took a sip of his now cold decaf coffee. Under the round dish in the centre of the table sat a pile of construction paper and a pair of scissors.

With a pencil and a ruler, he made a grid on paper that ran thirty squares down and twenty-five across. Inside each square, he wrote numbers ranging from zero to 100 in differing combinations until the grid was full. He then cut the squares into pairs, folded them, and stapled them shut.

Outside, he labeled each a number starting with one up to fifty. Then, he placed all of them inside a blue bank deposit bag he had got from his short stint as a bank janitor before he got laid off.

After setting it aside, he moved to a new page in his notebook, pulled out his cell phone, and started making his weekly calls to everyone he knew to see if they were interested in tickets for the night's game. While doing so, he wrote down their names until he sold every ticket.

The rest of the day, he would spend at home leisurely watching television as he waited for people to come by and drop off the money for the tickets. Sometimes he would need to make a trip down to where they worked because they wouldn't always be able to come to his house with the money. One such person was David Alvarado.

David sometimes worked as a line cook at Benny's and often made Santos make the trip over to the restaurant. Being in his mid-twenties, he was a frequent buyer. David already committed to $100 worth of tickets, and this transaction alone made the trip worth it. Santos sat at the counter and waved David over, who was in the back kitchen. He wasn't that much taller than Santos and had short shaggy dark black hair that seemed unkept, but David swore he had styled it. David normally sported two silver hoop earrings, but Benny's made him take them off during his shift.

The lack of facial hair minus a razor thin moustache that one would have to strain to see always made Santos chuckle whenever he saw him. Santos could never really understand David's style of rotating rock band tee shirts and ridiculously tight all black jeans. Santos did like his Converse though, as he had a pair when he was around his age.

David took off his hairnet and apron and approached Santos. "Hey, Pops. How's your morning?"

As the clock approached noon, the restaurant filled up with customers. The backdrop displayed the monogram of "Good Food-Good Friends-Good Times" while honey-coloured hanging lamps hovered over each of the crowded tables with customers.

The clacking of shoes and heels resonated across the restaurant on the gray laminate floor. Even though it was nearing midday, the sun still peeked through the large, blinded windows on the opposite side of the counter near the front of the restaurant where Santos sat.

He always called Santos *Pops*. "Mijo, como estas. You just get in, huh?"

"I don't freaking get out of here till eight. Sucks I won't see the game. Doesn't matter, though."

David motioned the cross on his chest and placed his hands together and pointed up. "God's with me on this game tonight. I can feel it, yo."

David cracked a smile.

"Here man, for tonight's game."

David slipped the bills under his hand. Santos nervously chuckled.

"Gracias, I'll let you know when the game is over." Santos motioned to the cross as well.

"Good luck, mijo."

5

CARLOS SAT AT HIS DESK, GOING THROUGH HIS emails, checking for any updates on the Martinez case. Around the room, others focused on their own work while Rankin sat in his office alone, talking with someone on the phone. The other detectives at their desks seemed rather hard at work typing as if one a speed typing test, making Carlos feel self-conscious about his skills.

The constant clicking jarred him as he tried to read and reread his emails, causing him to read the same paragraph over several times. It was as if almost his brain was focusing on all the surrounding minutia instead of letting him focus.

Next came the far-off ringing of the desk phones and seemed to go unanswered, followed by Rankin's annoying little habit of saying "uhhu" after every other word on the phone. After the 10th "uhhu" and the millionth clicking and phone ringing, he completely lost his focus. Carlos then tried scrolling through the reports, but no updates had come in.

Suddenly, his desk phone rang and even though the display was blank, he answered it anyway. In the corner of his eye, he could see Rankin setup a fan in the office, which caused a breeze to linger down to the detective's pit. Even though he stopped smoking, the Pall Malls still loitered in the air.

"Detective Alvarado."

"Hi. I am trying to follow up on a case."

"How can I help you?"

"My name is Henry Morelo. Um, Santos Morelo is...*was* my father. I understand you're handling his case."

Carlos's legs began their nervous tap dance under his desk. With every bit of strength, he tried to stop it, but sometimes they had a mind of their own. "Mr. Morelo. I don't believe I gave you my full name. It's Detective Carlos Alvarado. I don't know if you remember me, but..."

"Carlos Alvarado? Oh, my god. CJ! When did you become a cop? Sorry, I meant, Detective. When did that happen?"

Carlos' legs stopped tapping and the tension in his shoulders relaxed. Sliding down his chair halfway before speaking, trying to hide his nervousness even though Henry was not physically present. Sometimes his anxiety took strange routes.

"You still remember my nickname. CJ or Carlos is fine. You don't need to call me 'Detective.' It's still kind of weird hearing that in front of my name." Carlos tapped his foot under his desk again.

"After I finished my undergrad at Valley Tech, the world seemed a lot different after Amanda died and I felt it was my duty to protect people, so I joined the academy. Five months later, I was a cop, and three years later, a detective."

"Wow, CJ, that's amazing. I am so proud of you. I'm glad you found something that makes you happy. Honestly, I am. So, all of this is because of your sister's death?"

"Not exactly, more like the catalyst. It drove me to change my life in a different direction to help people differently. It just felt like the right thing to do."

"Whatever the reason, I'm glad it worked out for you."

Carlos could hear the weird combination of grief and excitement in Henry's voice and wasn't sure how Henry was holding it together. Losing a parent was something Carlos never went through, luckily. Carlos had seen it around him over the years, but it never affected him directly and wasn't sure how to comfort Henry. Plus, he had the added pressure of Henry being his ex and trying to corral his feelings and being professional.

"You know, the reason I called you is because of my father. After Detective Salinas called me and told me the news, I headed down from Denton. I hadn't even talked to my dad in years, and we weren't all that close, but someone had to show up for him. When I got home, I looked around the house and it felt empty. Extra quiet. I found myself in the kitchen just staring at how unused it looked."

"Henry, I know how painful losing someone close to you can be. If you need to talk, I'll be here. Not just in an official capacity, either."

"Thanks. When Detective Salinas mentioned someone had poisoned my father, I was in shock. My mind raced and locked up at the same time. I mean, who would want to do that to someone at my father's age? I mean, poisoned, really? Just seems so strange."

Carlos tilted his head to the side.

"It is something we are looking into. Keep in mind that this is only a preliminary autopsy report, and further tests are being done, including a full toxicology report. I need you to be patient with us. If you like, I can come over in an hour and walk you through what we have so far?"

"That would be perfect. I'll see you soon."

Carlos closed his emails and viewed the toxicology report one more time before meeting Henry to get his information up to date. The report was preliminary and wasn't complete, but indicated Mr. Morelo's heart medication from his medical records was missing in his bloodstream. It would be at least a couple of days before the eventual results came back.

Carlos doubted his over eagerness in offering to come over to Henry's home. Walking the tightrope of police work and friendship was tricky. Carlos hadn't shared Henry's and his history with Rankin, but to Carlos it had been eons ago when they had been kids. Could it really *matter*?

What mattered to Carlos was finding justice and nothing would impede that.

Carlos pulled up to Henry's. Carlos didn't notice it before, but now he heard the rampant sounds of cicadas emanating all around him. It made him feel like he was walking into a swamp. Most of the lights were off except one coming from the back porch. Henry answered the door and extended his hand. Carlos noticed that his own hands were clammy, and his eyes avoided Henry's gaze.

It had been a long time. Almost eight years passed. Henry was wearing a plain black shirt and some dark blue jeans and a lot more tattoos. A large "M" etched into the right forearm. Those eyes spoke before he did. Carlos' fading memories of Henry always included black painted nails and gauges or plugs in his ears, but he had none in the present. Although his skin seemed darker than before, could it be that north Texas had more sun than Valley City?

"CJ, come in, come in. Sorry, it's so dark. I was on the back porch, taking in the night. Come join me."

Henry motioned him in and to the back.

"It's nice back here."

"It's kind of peaceful. I like that, you know."

Carlos's neck was still giving him some pain. Adjusting his neck, made it snap and pop this time. Out back, he found an oasis of green. The divided lawn smelled recently cut and dewy moisture that dripped from the grass made the air resonate with the smell of tilled soil.

The palm trees lining the canal just outside of his yard swayed in the wind, giving way to the cracking and popping of palm fronds as they made way down to the ground. Henry's porch had a rundown couch to sit on that upon sitting on blew a smoke bomb sized gust of dust up and around Carlos, exchanging the CK One he had on for the dust bowl of his couch. Carlos just grinned, but Henry hardly noticed.

"Gee, are you feeling alright? Cracking your neck like that seems like it would hurt."

Carlos smiled. "Naw, I'm used to it by now. I must have slept wrong again. It's no biggie."

They made their way over to the couch and sat down facing the nearby canal.

"I'm glad you came over. I appreciate it. You mentioned that the tests done on my father were preliminary. What does that even mean?"

Inside his head, Carlos' imaginary hamster cage was running at full speed. It was not the most comfortable conversation to have with anyone. Henry, being his ex, made it even worse. Carlos slowed his breathing before speaking in order to calm his nerves.

"We found traces of rat poison, but the tests were inconclusive. We are running more tests to determine exactly what was in his blood. It will take a few days."

"I hope you let me know what's going on once you hear more?"

"Of course."

"It's just been kind of hard not knowing... I hate being in the dark."

Carlos could empathize. Not knowing or not being in control was one of his pet peeves. Being a detective, it always made him look closer for missed clues. Being on the other side of the investigation was a whole other matter.

"Henry, I get where you're coming from. It's the not knowing that sucks. The constant worrying about how things are coming along. I'll do my best to keep you in the loop every step of the way."

Carlos noticed Henry was jiggling his knee repeatedly, so he lightly touched Henry's knee, an impulse, muscle memory. Carlos immediately regretted doing it and probably had gone too far in trying to comfort Henry, making his heart sink.

"You're still doing that, huh? It always was your giveaway, since it's something we share. We could never hide our feelings from each other because of it."

"You were always the more observant one. I guess that's why you became a cop, huh?"

"It's going to be alright. I promise I'll do everything I can to find out what happened to your father. You have my word on that."

Henry's facial muscles relaxed, and he was no longer avoiding eye contact. The man seemed more at ease.

"You never broke a promise."

Carlos wanted to smile, but he didn't want Henry to misinterpret it. Touching his knee brought a flood of mixed emotions to the surface. It felt like a warm cup of hot chocolate at bedtime: his definition of comfort.

"Before I head out, I need to ask you about a couple of things I found when I did my walkthrough the other day."

Carlos pulled out his phone and tabbed over to the photos app, scooting closer to Henry on the couch, letting their knees touch for an instant before separating.

"Here, you see this business card for Treasure Hills Graphics? Does the name sound familiar to you, or have you ever heard your father talking about them?"

"Honestly, my father and I hadn't talked in almost ten

years. So, if he was involved with that business, I wouldn't know. Why, do you think it means something or has something to do with his death?"

"It's too early to tell. I just wanted to ask because it was one of the few things I found in his room."

Carlos paused for a beat and wasn't too sure how to bring up the thousands of dollars stashed under his bed, figuring the direct approach was best.

"One of the things? You found something else?"

"Flip to the next picture. I found *that* hidden under your father's bed in a cash lockbox. I didn't count it, but there had to be close to several thousand. Any idea where your father would have gotten that kind of cash? He was retired, right? From the digging I did, I found he was living on his social security benefit monthly. It wasn't much, but I couldn't find any other trace of income."

"That's a lot of money CJ to be hiding under his bed and not in a bank account. The only thing I could think of was his betting pool. Do you know about that?"

"Not sure that I follow you."

"My father was running a local sports betting pool for high school and other football games. Growing up, he used to do that a lot. I guess he never stopped. Maybe because he would rake in several hundred dollars a week, so if you put two and two together..."

"Right, now I get you. Thanks for the information. I will add that piece of information to the file, but I will need you later to add to your statement, if you don't mind."

"No problem. Is the money still there?"

"No, we tagged it as evidence; it's in holding, pending the investigation. I just thought I'd ask you about it on the off chance you might've known. I'll follow up with the graphics shop lead as well and let you know if I find anything else."

Carlos scratched the back of his neck, knowing it wasn't

kosher to ask Henry out, given their history and adding to the fact that he was on duty, so he didn't know how to broach the subject. Carlos heard the crashing of the water against the canal banks almost like a beating heart pulsing. He turned to face him before speaking.

"I know that you're still going through a lot and can only imagine how it must be going through all of it alone. If you wouldn't mind the company, I was wondering if you might want to get together later for drinks and to play catch up when I'm not here in an official capacity. I want to be there for you."

Carlos paused.

"Just friends, ok?"

"Why not," hoarsely said Henry.

Carlos' shoulders and body language changed and seemed to lighten as a smile broke the worrisome look on his face.

"I didn't mean to catch you off guard there Henry, but I gotta say that's the cutest sounding yes I've ever gotten before. We can go to Dan's tomorrow. It's their Drag Bingo night. You remember Dan's, right?"

"It's ok. I could use a night away from this house. I don't really feel comfortable here."

"I'll call you tomorrow."

Carlos used the side entrance to leave. Henry waved to him as he disappeared around the corner. Someone turned off the porch light and the lights inside the home. Carlos had always been adept at keeping his professional and personal life separate until Henry returned to Valley City.

Even after the near decade, those feelings that he had let go because of his fear were still there, and managing them was going to be tricky. If there was one thing Carlos knew how to do was walk a tightrope of work life balance. He learned that from continually working on his sister's cold case. Their meetup would be interesting.

The fence he was walking inside his head teetered under

the pressure. Sitting in his truck, the surrounding quietness grew. For a neighbourhood so densely packed, there was hardly any stirring about. The only thing he could hear were the frogs and crickets from the nearby canal.

His truck engine broke the silence, roaring back to life. Carlos really hated obeying the speed limits, and even though something told him to get home soon because he needed all the rest he could get, he continued to drive at a leisurely pace.

Tomorrow, the actual work would begin.

6

Santos arrived early to get his usual seat. In his old age, he could still walk on his own, but his eyesight was something that gave him trouble. His glasses were black rimmed and plastic and very simple, much like Santos. From head to toe, Santos never really dressed more than the basics. He liked to wear his walking Sketchers, his work Dickie pants, and most of the time a Guayabera, the Mexican traditional short sleeve embroidered shirt or a Cowboys jersey. He was a man of extremes, either formal or very causal.

The Treasure Hills Pirates were playing against the Westbrook Giants. He sat on the Treasure Hills side. The long metal bleachers had no padding and usually caused Santos back aches, which is why he brought along a small cushion. Small metal handrails that often were wobbly upon touch and sometimes broke off because of rust divided the twenty plus rows. Santos was aware not to touch them from experience.

The game already started, and the crowd seemed to rally for the Pirates. Both sides of the field could hear loud cheers. Treasure Hills had upgraded the stadium since last Santos had visited because a brand-new score board stood at Treasure

Hills end zone with the largest screen he had ever seen. It reminded him of the ones he saw on tv when he watched the Cowboys play. Even the astroturf seemed an extra shade of green, almost too bright. All this told Santos that Treasure Hills lived up to its namesake and was carrying money to spare.

Santos didn't really know any of the players, nor did he care much about who won. He was there to sell the rest of his tickets. The ones left included the caveat of being half-time tickets. It meant the score on the ticket had to matchup at halftime, so people still had chances to purchase them.

Santos peered across the crowd and found two cops hanging around the gate entrance on the far side of the stadium. What he was doing wasn't exactly legal, but it wasn't illegal either. With the cops occupied, he sold as many tickets as he could before halftime. When he was done, the money was secure in his wallet, and the game was nearing the middle. He took a break for a coffee at the food stands.

When Santos descended into the food stands under the bleachers, he found a long line. Besides the food stands, there wasn't much down there. Pockets of dark spots dotted the length of the bleachers and culminated next to the restrooms. There wasn't much traffic at the restrooms, so Santos excused himself from the line and headed over.

He used the restroom in hopes the line would be shorter when he returned. The closer he got to the restrooms, the darker and less lit it got. Despite the dull noise from above his head, Santos picked up on some muffled sounds coming from the restrooms. There was a sign that showed it was a single-use restroom, yet he could hear multiple voices coming from inside. The sounds got louder, yet he still could not decipher what they were.

A snapping sound came from the door as it unlocked, and two individuals exited. They seemed to be in a hurry, but before they could leave the poorly lit area, Santos recognized the second individual. It was David. Having a hard time seeing in the dark because of his poor vision, he saw into the restroom and glimpses the mirror.

Seeing his own reflection and now David's side by side, he didn't know how similar in skin tone they were. Santos was darker than most Mexicans because of the Native American blood in his family, but that's where the similarity ended. Santos' thick arm hair, bushy beard, and long sideburns easily could have confused him for the Wolfman, despite his lack of hair on his head. That's why he usually wore his Cowboys cap.

"What you doing?" asked Santos in broken English.

David's eyes sank, and he blushed.

"Pops, what am I doing? What are you doing down here, scaring me like that?" said David, attempting to skirt the question.

"Mijo, I was just waiting for the restroom, y tu (and you)?"

"Look, Pops, it's nothing you gotta worry about. I gotta go but reach out to me later about the tickets to see how I did," David blurted out as he dashed out of the area and back upstairs to the bleachers, leaving Santos no time to respond.

Santos entered the restroom to use the facilities when he noticed a strong tinge in the air. There was an almost metallic aroma, accompanied by a lighter and sweeter scent. Santos didn't want to believe it, but he recognized the odour.

As he finished and went over to the sink to wash his hands, a crackling sound came from under his shoes. He found glass pieces in the shape of a thin cylinder. Parts of it seemed to be coated in something that looked like white powdery residue. He would get to the bottom of this.

Back home, he made the calls to the ticket winners and let them know when they could come and pick up their share of the pot. David was not among the winners, yet he still needed to call him. Santos didn't want to seem intrusive in David's life, but over the course of the last several months, he thought they grew close enough that a concerned phone call to him wouldn't seem out of the ordinary.

Before making the call, he made himself a cup of decaf coffee. He added his two scoops of creamer and sweet n' low and mixed it vigorously. He took two giant gulps and left the rest to cool. Santos sat down at the kitchen table and called David.

"David, it's Santos. I just wanted to call and give you an update on your tickets. You didn't do so well, but one ticket gained you twenty bucks. You can grab them whenever."

"Shit, Pops, that sucks. Fuck it, it's enough for a twenty of," David said, then caught himself and stopped speaking.

"It's not my place to pry, but what was going on inside the restroom earlier?"

"I told you, Pops. It's really nothing for you to worry about. I mean, you gotta lay off me. You gotta trust me."

David's rate of speech sped up.

"I found the glass pieces inside. So, you had to be doing drugs. What kinds, I don't know. All I care about is you being safe and not hurting yourself."

"Shit, Pops, drugs. You sound like some Telenovela going to extremes and exaggerating."

"I'm exaggerating?"

David took a beat before speaking.

"Look, I was doing a little T, but I got it under control. I don't do it every day, okay? You feel better now that I've told you. Will you trust me now?"

"T? Que es eso?"

"T, Tina. It's meth, Pops. You know?"

"Hijole, meth, David. I don't know what to say right now."

Santos was beside himself and couldn't eke out another word.

"Look, calm down. It's okay. Therefore, I didn't wanna tell you. You're going to blow it out of proportion. You really don't get it. I'm good. I promise you."

David coughed several times before catching his breath.

"I'll pick up that twenty tomorrow morning. I'll call before heading over..."

David continued to cough, but this time, it didn't seem to stop.

"David, estas bien? Are you ok?"

David didn't answer, but with more coughs and what sounded like phlegm being expelled repeatedly. Santos was worrying more when David was not answering. As the phlegm subsided, the coughing increased, David tried to get a word in.

"I...gotta...go." David didn't answer Santos and instead just hung up, leaving Santos imagining the worst.

7

THE MORNING AFTER HE VISITED HENRY, CARLOS left the station and headed across town to Treasure Hills. The neighbourhood association boasted that "none of their houses went for under a million dollars."

Carlos always found it funny how the people who lived there thought of themselves as something of a higher caliber. Treasure Hills got its name from the winding slopes and hills that surround the neighbourhood and lined the various streets. Most people thought these hills were a natural formation for Valley City, but how could they be? Farmlands and canals adorned most of the city, lacking any notable elevation.

The only reason Treasure Hills maintained its elevation was because of what was below its surface. Thirty years ago, the neighbourhood stood on the exact spot where Valley City's municipal landfill is now located. The city used the landfill for decades until it reached its maximum capacity and became unusable.

A few years after decommissioning, Related Company from out of state sought to repurpose the land into a shiny fresh development boasting its own schools, parks, and retail spaces. It took several years to get the approval from the city, but in 1994, Treasure Hills development was chartered, and ground breaking occurred. Four years later, they completed the first section of the neighbourhood, and so on.

Nowadays, no one could even tell a landfill used to sit where their favourite coffee shop now brews their fancy morning lattes. Carlos couldn't help but think Treasure Hills had something to hide since its façade of wealthy neighbourhoods was one of a literal coverup. Trash covered by wealth. Most people don't even remember that part of its history.

Carlos approached the entrance gate and guardhouse of the neighbourhood. The guard at the entrance gate checked his credentials and granted him access. He found the graphics shop on the corner of Treasure Hills Boulevard and Madison Avenue.

There was a single car parked outside of the shop. However, there was no foot traffic, despite it being only eleven in the morning. Before exiting his car, he made sure not to forget his notepad and pen. The shop's sign stood out in bright green and yellow lettering. The glass door read RUBEN DELGADO; OWNER etched in white font.

Inside, he found the simple space smaller than he had expected. Several chairs lined the entrance in a makeshift waiting area, and the service counter seemed bare. There was a sole computer on the counter where the cash register and a letter holder with a stack of invoices were located. Behind the counter were piles and piles of clear storage containers with various colours of T-shirts labeled with sizes and other markers. Everything looked organized, yet no one was around. The silence was almost unnerving.

The only other room in the building had a door that was labeled PRIVATE and EMPLOYEES ONLY. The door had a separate deadbolt that someone could lock from the inside. Carlos took the time to make a note of this anomaly. He saw one tiny camera in the back corner that was pointed toward the front door, and its little red light was blinking. This meant it was broadcasting somewhere. Carlos thought it must be in the back room.

Carlos took out his badge and tapped it on the counter. "Hello, Valley City PD. Is anyone here?"

A slight shuffling noise came from the other side of the door in the backroom. A garbled voice spoke, but was unintelligible. The backdoor clicked and twisted, and someone exited.

The individual screamed with surprise but also a tinge of annoyance. From what Carlos assumed must be the proprietor of the business, stood a lanky but well-built man with muscles poking out of his one size too small v neck shirt which stood in contrast to his scruffiness of his facial hair that didn't seem to connect to his moustache. In polar opposite were his pleated black slacks and leather belt with the shiniest pair of dress shoes Carlos had ever seen. This man was a walking contradiction.

"Good morning. Sorry, I was working on inventory, and you literally caught me elbow deep in paperwork." The man stood at normal a height of five foot nine inches and had watchful eyes that seemed to scan the room repeatedly.

His most distinguished feature being slick black hair parted to the right, almost shining in the abundance of hair goop, making his appearance greasy and his middle age more apparent. He wiped his hands on his pants before extending his hand out and pulling his shirt in place.

"Morning. My name is Detective Alvarado from Valley PD, and I'm investigating the death of one of your patrons. Could you answer some questions?"

The individual's eyes shifted away from Carlos; his lips

seemed chapped. He stood on the other side of the divider between the back workshop and lobby.

"Of course, I'm sorry I didn't introduce myself; my name is Ruben Delgado. I'm the owner. Sorry, you said this was about one of my clients—who died?"

"His name was Santos Morelo. Do you recall him?"

Ruben's whole body sunk, and his demeanour changed.

"Oh, my gosh, poor Santos. Of course, I knew him. We had done business the last several years, ever since he coached the Police Officer's Charity Softball League. But I suppose you know that part."

Carlos scribbled a note.

"Right, of course. Continue, please."

"Like I said, when he became coach, I did all the uniforms for the team every year, and since the league was for charity, I donated my services and materials. It was the least I could do. I always like to help my community when I can." Ruben pointed out several displays on the wall that showcased past uniforms and shirts he made for the team, along with pictures of past baseball teams in full uniform.

Ruben's eyes turned to the computer screen when it made a beeping sound. Ruben moved the mouse around, attempting to stop the noise, to no avail.

"Is there something wrong, Mr. Delgado?"

"Not at all. I have a ton of work to get back to. It's my quarterly inventory. It usually takes me all day. I dread it every time. Was there anything else?"

"A couple of more questions. I won't take much more of your time. So, besides the softball league, you had no other business with Mr. Morelo?"

"No, not really."

Carlos stopped writing in his notepad and looked Ruben directly in the eyes.

"No, or not really. It can't be both."

Ruben turned off the computer.

"Now and then, I would buy a football ticket from him."

Carlos closed his notebook and adjusted his stance toward the half door entrance into the workroom. "What you mean, a football ticket?"

"He ran these betting pools weekly for local high school football games. The ticket you could buy had a score, and a quarter listed on it. If the score matched your ticket, you would win the pot. Sometimes it got up to two-three hundred dollars."

"Mr. Delgado, I'm not here about Mr. Morelo's betting pool, but steer clear of anything like that in the future."

Carlos placed his notepad back in his pocket.

"I just mentioned it because you asked. Heard enough?"

"I don't really think any of this is something to take lightly, especially Mr. Morelo's death. We still haven't ruled out any foul play, and I'm leaving all my options on the table. Do you understand me, Mr. Delgado?"

"Right, I do."

Ruben walked across the counter and headed toward the front entrance. Before he opened the front door, a light thud came from the back room.

"What was that? Is there someone else back here? It's best if you are straight with me."

Carlos began walking toward the back room with his gun drawn.

"I'm telling you the truth. I'm alone."

"In that case, you won't mind if I look in the back room for just a second?"

"I have nothing to hide. Go ahead."

Ruben moved toward the backroom and opened the door.

Carlos clicked his safety off and slowly entered the backroom. There were stacks of printer paper boxes and several filing cabinets with tags and writing on them. In the corner stood a desk and a workspace with a small futon. The walls were 70s wood paneling. Carlos saw no one in the room. Ruben's computer monitor had a video feed of the other room. It only confirmed the camera that he saw earlier. He made one last sweep of the room before heading back to the front entrance. He holstered his gun back.

"You can never be too careful. Thank you for your cooperation, and if you can think of anything else which might help me in my investigation, call me."

Carlos exited and remained in his car for a moment as he collected his thoughts into his notepad. Something was off and wasn't sure how to proceed. He didn't want to appear strong, but he also didn't want to give up completely. He turned on his truck and took a drive around the corner. From his vantage point, as he crossed Treasure Hills Boulevard and into 1st Street, he saw Ruben's shop had an extensive alleyway presence.

As he turned his truck into the nearest alley and made his way there, he noticed a camera pointing toward the back entrance. There were no outside windows, and the camera's lights didn't seem to be on.

In case the cameras had been working, he remained out of view and parked near a post office parking lot behind a few cars. He waited. Ruben had something to hide. Perhaps it was his resistance to Carlos' questions, or it could have been his restlessness.

An hour passed, and with no signs of activity, Carlos came back later. He wanted to get started on running some background on Ruben and his business. Just as he was about to leave, he noticed movement through the back entrance. He saw Ruben exit and hug someone that seemed to be in a rush. The individual was wearing a black overcoat and a black baseball cap, undoubtedly trying to avoid being seen.

Carlos waited to see what would happen, but only two

minutes later, an Uber approached and took the individual away. Carlos had to decide to either stay and observe Ruben further or follow the individual in the Uber. He wrote the license plate and followed up on the car later.

For now, he wanted to monitor Ruben to see what kind of traffic his business received. There had to be clues. It was up to him to find them.

Ruben watched Carlos leave, locked the front entrance, and flipped the open sign to close before heading into the backroom. Inside, he found it as he left it. He grabbed a flathead screwdriver from his drawer and moved the couch off to the side. He placed the screwdriver in between one of the wall panels and flicked it open. A door about waist high opened, and inside, David rushed out of the crawl space. In his hand, he had a glass pipe wrapped in a green bandana with a lighter all bundled together. David's eyes were red and sweat poured from his forehead.

"Fuck, that was too close, babe. I mean, my brother almost caught us. How did he fucking find out about us, anyway?"

David cleaned the bottom of the glass pipe, lit the lighter under it, and took a lung full of the meth.

"Calm down. He wasn't here looking for you. He came to ask me about some guy that died. I did business with him in the past. Santos Morchello or something?"

Ruben motioned for the pipe as he took a hit as well.

"Morelo, you mean? Santos Morelo?"

"You knew him?"

Ruben placed the pipe on his desk.

"I knew Mr. Morelo. He was a good guy. Whenever I was in a bind, he was always there to help me. He would always spot me when I was low on cash."

David eyed the ground.

"Spot you cash? What like a sugar daddy?"

"Not like that, you fucker. There's only one daddy in my life."

David grabbed Ruben at the waist and kissed him deeply. Ruben slid off David's shirt and unbuttoned his jeans, landing on the couch. Their night just began.

8

Carlos passed Valley City High School and its palm tree laden canals along the way to Dan's Bar. Dan's was at the corner of Ware Road and La Vista street. Sitting in its parking lot was Mac's Taco truck. That was not always present and must have appeared since Carlos's last visit.

Beyond the rust-coloured walls of the bar, lines of suburban homes surrounded it, all matching in colour and shape. It would seem uniformity had been important to its designers and not uniqueness, unlike Dan's Bar, which prided itself on being like nothing else around. Of course, there were other gay bars in the area, but none lasted as long as Dan's.

The atmosphere hadn't changed one bit as Carlos pulled into the parking lot. There was no parking attendant in sight, and only a handful of spaces remained. The lack of spaces made Carlos' pulse race and cause his anxiety to rise. The previous occurrence of a mini attack similar to this happened ages ago when Henry and he ended their relationship in high school. It was less actual anxiety and more of the walls closing in on him emotionally. Carlos' emotions were never one to have much stability anyway, but over the years, they have grown less erratic. But during high school, while he had been dating Henry, they were the most erratic.

***

GRADUATION WAS ONLY TWO MONTHS AWAY AND Carlos was excited to be heading off to UNT with Henry. They were dating for the entire school year, but for Carlos it seemed like an eternity already and couldn't wait to spend four years of college with Henry in north Texas.

Everything was in place, the applications, the financial aid, and even the dorm room assignments they received as roommates. Henry's parents purchased a car for him and Carlos to use for their move to north Texas. Everything was in place but as time passed, Carlos felt his anxiety rising and emotional state teeter.

He was conscious of his genuine feelings for Henry and there was nothing more he desired than to spend the next four years with him, but he sensed an unsettling feeling, and it was increasing. After a while, even Henry noticed, and it came to a head on the day before graduation when Carlos' last official checklist item was to pick up their cap and gown from the graduation committee's office. After securing the items, he drove over to meet Henry at the Hygeia Dairy Bar for some congratulatory milkshakes.

As he pulled up to the ice cream parlour in all its bright white glory, that reminded one of a bygone time long gone where delivery men brought your milk to your front door. There didn't seem to be much foot traffic, and inside the ice cream parlour, Henry could be seen swirling a spoon inside a milkshake glass and glancing at his watch. The attendant seemed to chat with him, and they both seemed engaged enough in conversation.

At that moment, Carlos realized there was nothing left to

do, no other errand, no next step, except graduate and move to north Texas. His breathing became erratic. The literal car doors seemed to squish and close in on him. Even the sunlight burned his eyes and gave him a pounding headache. Carlos wanted it to stop and realized all this time he was just too afraid to leave Valley City.

It never dawned on him before to leave before meeting Henry and always thought their relationship was a fluke and wouldn't last but here they were ten months later getting ready to leave Valley City with no real desire to leave and Carlos had no way to tell Henry to the truth so instead he told the worst kind of lie.

Carlos walked into the parlour and flagged Henry over. There was a tv in the background playing random music videos and a few older people chatting in the corner. Carlos waved away the attendant, not ordering something when Henry tackled a hug into me.

"Babe, you finally got here! You got the cap and gown?"

By this point, Carlos was no longer smiling. "Yep, all set."

"Um, what's wrong?"

"Why do you think something is wrong?"

"Now I know something is wrong. You're deflecting."

Carlos rolled his eyes. "I really wished you wouldn't have taken that psychology elective."

"I'm being serious CJ, what's wrong?"

Carlos was limited in time to think of what to say to Henry, but based on their conversations over the months, the aspect that constantly bothered him about other couples, and particularly his parents' relationship, was infidelity. He hated cheaters with a passion and would never take one back. It was an easy out, but it would unnecessarily hurt Henry. A divided decision Carlos would later feel remorseful about.

"I cheated. Don't ask with who. They don't even go to our school. I met them during Spring Break when we went to

South Padre Island for the weekend. You went to eat dinner with your uncle and his wife, and I stayed behind because I had food poisoning. Well, I lied. I snuck off and met the guy and, well, I don't need to go into detail. I'm sorry."

"CJ, I...I mean, how...you know what? You know what you gave up and I hope one day you know what you will look back and see how much you have wronged me, but much more how badly you have wronged yourself. Goodbye CJ."

Carlos stayed inside the parlour as he watched Henry get into his car and leave and disappear into the winding neighbourhood. It was impulsive and reckless, but all the anxiety and tension had disappeared. The walls receded. The levee was nowhere near breaking, but at what cost?

THESE WANDERING THOUGHTS WASHED OVER Carlos as he viewed the gas station across the street, which still had their signs of NO PARKING. WILL TOW AT OWNERS EXPENSE. That too didn't changed.

As he opened the gray warehouse-like doors, a smell he almost forgotten hit Carlos in the face: desperation and vodka. Upon scanning the room, he observed most of the people congregated around the newly transformed Bingo tables. The organizers stripped the stage where the drag queens usually performed and replaced it with a table and bingo ball hopper for the evening. The staff pushed all the usual cocktail tables off to the side and towards the back of the bar, giving the bingo floor a little more room to work with.

Carlos noticed that Dan's opened the patio off to the side where Mac's Taco Truck was, which made it pretty convenient to grab a bite when, inevitability, a drunk would get hungry. Hanging multi-coloured string lights and a handful of Japanese paper lanterns illuminated the patio, which caught

Carlos's attention. The music, which normally was louder than the thoughts inside your head, was at a comfortable level while the bingo stage was being set up. People were scattered across the stage in various table setups.

Each table had stacks of bingo cards and a box filled with bingo markers. A handful of people were still hanging out by the bar, including the same bartender Carlos last seen there, Alfonso. Most of the conversation buzz came from the bar area.

Carlos walked over to the bar to order, wondering if Alfonso would recognize him. Years later, Alfonso still looked nearly the same, but now he was sporting a gray manicured goatee and a graying head of black hair. Muscles bulged from his tight Dan's T-shirt. Alfonso placed a bar napkin in front of Carlos.

"Hola compadre, eres tu Carlos?" Alfonso opened the bar flap and rushed toward Carlos to hug him.

"Alfonso, good to see you. Can't believe you remember me. It's been almost... ten years?"

"Si, si mas o menos pero still good to see you. You still drink Old Fashion?"

"Impressive. Yeah, give me one."

Alfonso made his magic happen behind the bar while Carlos tactically browsed the room in search of Henry. Luck was not on his side. The bartender placed his drink in front of him.

"There you go, Mr. Carlos. The first one is on the house. So, you have a date or estas solo esta noche?"

"I'm meeting someone, but I'm not sure where he is. He's my ex, but I'm helping him on a case I'm working on."

Alfonso's eyes pulled back and his face gave Carlos the impression he was trying to search for the words in English, but they didn't come to him. Most of the crowd made their way to the bingo tables. From the reflection in the bar mirrors, he observed the stage being prepared and a trio of drag queens getting ready through a crack in the dressing room door.

"I'm a cop now. We were supposed to meet to catch up."

"Oh, congrats senor. Es exciting, I bet. You said you are waiting for an ex, no? You mean the man you used to come here with? Como se llama, Henry?"

"That's him. Did you see him? Is he here?" Carlos twisted head back and around looking for Henry. Big Love by Fleetwood Mac was playing over the sound system. Alfonso possessed an exceptional memory.

"Oh yes, he was here pero se fue al bano. There he comes out," Alfonso said as he pointed toward the bathroom.

Carlos swivelled his seat and saw Henry exit the bathroom. Henry was wearing black jeans, a Valley City Walkathon T-shirt from 2010, and a blue backward baseball cap. Despite having seen him the night before, a distinct sensation arose upon seeing him in the company of others, causing his stomach to sink and his hands to grow clammy. Did he genuinely still have emotions for Henry?

When their eyes met, Carlos wanted to run over to him and give him a hug, but he didn't want to seem desperate. Instead, he waited for him to come over to him. As Henry embraced him, the scent of bleach and Coors Light surrounded Carlos. He tried not to hold on to him for too long, but realized his hug already went on longer than he intended.

Carlos released his grip and pulled out a stool for Henry.

"You've got some manners there," said Henry while staring at Carlos's drink.

"I already ordered. Would like you something? I've got a tab open."

"Um, I think I'm in the mood for vodka. So, let me get a greyhound."

"Alfonso, can you—"

"No worries, Mr. Carlos." Alfonso extended his hand out to Henry. "Mr. Henry, good to see you. A greyhound, you said?" Henry nodded.

Carlos tapped his foot on the bar stool and knocked his knees against the bar several times. He couldn't comprehend the reason behind his nervousness in Henry's presence. Carlos really began wondering if his feelings, long unattended, had resurfaced.

When Carlos hit his knee on the bar again, it made him think of the other night when he had held Henry's knee. They had said little about it, but Carlos could almost feel Henry through the tips of his fingers. The music seemed to fade slowly, and his inner voice grew louder. He could hear himself thinking and wondering if he should do something similar.

Carlos focused his vision on the mirror and watched Mac, the bar back, finish setting up the tables. From the side room, he could see drag queens peeking out, checking out the crowd. Seeing a drag queen in full getup is one thing, but in half drag is another. He caught a glimpse of an unnamed queen peeking out without full makeup, her wig, and dressed in a red robe. Carlos made eye contact with her for a moment, and the queen shut the door.

When he looked back at Henry, he was staring directly at him with a corner lipped smile.

"Hi," Carlos said, while studying his facial expressions. Henry seemed to be in a good mood, despite everything going on around him.

"Hi back." Henry smirked.

"Are we gonna play bingo or just hang out here? Up to you."

Carlos sipped his drink.

Carlos hadn't stopped to think about playing or not. That would throw off how he had envisioned the night would go, and he preferred to be prepared for all possibilities.

"It would be more fun if we chilled here at the bar where we can talk some more. That's how I feel, anyway. Why don't we move over to the booth in the corner?"

"Good idea."

Carlos moved his bar stool out. Henry gave him a little nudge, and they walked over to the one of the empty back booths. The lights were dimmer, and the music was less in your face. As they slid into the same side of the booth, their bodies connected again. Carlos grazed Henry's pinky.

"This seems like a better spot to talk," Carlos said.

Henry nodded. Carlos was now in an enclosed space, a more private space with Henry. It made him nauseous and excited at the same. The evening wasn't going as he planned in his head. It was going better. Before they spoke, the event organizers introduced Valerie Paris, the emcee for the evening, who performed her signature song, "Man! I Feel Like a Woman!"

After her set, the bingo game began, and Carlos moved his attention back to Henry. Carlos noticed their drinks had emptied. He flagged over Alfonso for some refills. Mac instead brought over the drinks while Alfonso kept busy behind the bar.

"Thanks for suggesting we come out tonight. I hadn't really left the house since everything happened. Even back in Denton, I didn't go out much. I hibernated at home. I went to class, work, and came back home. Depressing now that I hear myself say it out loud."

"We all get set in our ways, and it becomes hard to break out of our patterns. If we do nothing different from what we do, how can we know there is something out there better for us?"

"I get you. It's just, I wasn't really expecting to be here again. So, when I got the call and found out that both my brother and sister had said they would not make it, I knew I had to come. Someone had to come and identify my father's body. I mean, what kind of people aren't willing to do that? It's pathetic, really."

Carlos chewed on his straw, listening attentively.

"Why didn't they want to come?"

"I tried calling them, but every time I do, it goes to voicemail. It's understandable they didn't answer my calls. I haven't spoken to them in four years. We just stopped talking."

Carlos wanted to ask for more detail, but he didn't want to push. He knew especially how hard it was to have siblings. Carlos figured he would tell him when he was ready.

Carlos could see from Henry's face and the quiver on his lips that he had wanted to say more, but again, he didn't want to broach the subject until Henry felt comfortable to do so. Then again, sometimes when he was in similar situations, all he wanted was someone to give him a little push to keep talking and just get his feelings out in the open. It had certainly helped him in the past.

"Henry, if you don't mind me asking, why did you stop talking to your siblings?"

The quiver on Henry's lip ceased and lines on his forehead scrunched up before he spoke.

"It's just that..." stuttered Henry then continuing, "well you know I came out really early in high school way before we ever went out like in my freshman year." Carlos nodded.

"I was fifteen years old, and my brother and sister were both five and ten years older than me. Obviously, they weren't living with my parents and I, but they came over on Sundays for dinner all the time. Every time they came over, it was the same thing. Hey Henry, did you repent and ask for forgiveness yet? Did you get the priest to pray the gay away? Can you believe that? They actually said that."

"That's horrible Henry. And your parents said nothing to them?"

"Not exactly. My parents weren't the happiest about me being gay, but at least they understood it was who I was. After a while, they told my brother and sister if they were going to be treating me that way, that they would be no longer welcome at our home and well that shut them up. But the thing is, it really hurt our relationship because after that, we just stopped trying to keep in touch. A day turned to weeks, turned to months, turned to years. So, I guess there is plenty of blame to go around."

"Regardless Henry, they shouldn't have treated you like that, especially being older than you. I'm just glad your parents stood up for you."

Carlos saw a glimmer of a smile crack Henry's face.

"Look, I'm going to change the subject. I don't feel like being a *Debbie Downer* anymore."

"It's ok. I don't mind you talking about your family. But I have some experience with tough sibling relationships. Do you remember my younger sister, Amanda?"

"I can't picture her face, but the name I remember. How come?"

Carlos hadn't shared Amanda's story with anyone in years. He hadn't said her name out loud in longer. It wasn't a competition, but he wanted Henry to know he understood grief, too.

"About six months after you left town, after I had graduated Valley Tech, my brother David and I went to the bar and left Amanda at home, studying and watching movies. It was something we did all the time. You understand there was no way for us to have known."

Carlos slowed his speech and paused for a moment.

"Known what?"

"We came home from the bar and found the front door to

the house open. There was a trail of blood going down the side of the house and to the front, near the mailbox. And that's where we found her."

For a brief second, Carlos pictured his sister's blood drenched over the front door trailing down the stairs. He could remember the iron stench of it and its stickiness under the doormat. Henry's smile dropped and his expression blanked, leaving Carlos unable to read it.

"Someone had stabbed her multiple times and left her there. No one stole or took anything. It didn't make any sense."

Carlos' eyes watered. Henry reached out to hug him. Carlos noticed Henry began to tear up, too. It was an unusual sight for two men to be at a bar crying in the dark corner while Shakira played. Carlos squeezed Henry's back and wiped his tears with his palm.

"I had no clue. God, that must be so hard. I'm so sorry. And did they find out who did it or what happened?"

"That's the shitty part. It's remained unsolved to this day. It's the reason I switched gears from being a teacher and joined the academy. I figured I could help and protect this shitty town and help others before something like that happens to someone else. That probably sounds kind of lame."

"Quite the opposite. I admire you. You saw something that needed changing, and you went out and made a difference and became a cop."

"I've had time to deal with it, and being a detective gives me the drive to continue. I enjoy helping people when they need the help the most."

Carlos noticed Henry's eyes had puffed up from crying. Empathy was something Carlos hardly saw in his line of work. It was nice to see Henry could still feel that after his father's death.

"Like you, Henry. I'm glad I'm able to help you with your father's case."

Henry cracked a smile. Carlos mimicked it.

"You know, it wasn't all gloomy. Even though my parents weren't exactly *there* for us, my mother, Amanda, and I spent time on the weekends making tamales together. I remember not really knowing what I was doing, but then again, I guess it didn't really matter. Looking back now, I'm sure my mom just wanted to spend time with us," Carlos said. His eyes glistened as he recalled the Sunday during Amanda's ninth birthday.

THE ALVARADO FAMILY KITCHEN STOOD unchanged in all the years that his parents owned it. The lime green vinyl floor had gray patches of various shapes resembling ink blots more than anything else. Honey oak cabinets circled the kitchen in a wraparound fashion, with off-white counters that could easily become dirty. On the centre island, the women in Carlos's life sat while he chopped and diced several pounds of chicken and pork.

"Why do we need so much meat, Mom?" asked Carlos.

Tucking her deep auburn hair into a ponytail, his mom halted stuffing tamales to speak. "You know I can't stuff and talk, mijo, but I'll make an exception since we are so far ahead, thanks to Mandy."

"Ma, I don't like when you call me Mandy. It sounds yucky."

"Ok, ok. Amanda. Better," said Carlos's mother as she directed her eyes toward Amanda.

Amanda nodded while the conversation continued. "We need so much meat because the tamales are not just for us. You know that during this time of year, we make extras for the church to give out during Easter service. I think this year we are making thirty dozen, so yes, it's a lot of meat, but it's for a good cause."

"I know, Mom, but still, it's a lot of work," Carlos said.

"Would you rather be outside helping your dad clean the RV for our trip?"

"Naw, I think I'd rather help you."

"Ma, how come you don't have a job?" said Amanda.

Carlos giggled as his mother answered.

"Well, I'm what you call a stay-at-home mom. It's my job to take care you, the boys, and the house. That's the only job I need."

"Maybe, one day when I'm older and have a family too, that can be my job too!"

"Seriously, Mandy, you don't need to suck up anymore. You're already getting a party and endless tamales," cracked Carlos.

"I told you; I don't like that name—just shut up!"

They would often cook together on Sundays, and now, reflecting on it, those were some of the most special times he had with his mom and sister, but it ended all too soon.

"CJ, that reminds me of when my dad and I would cook beans on the weekends. My mother left us to do all the cooking, which I didn't mind. It was the only time we got to spend time with each other," said Henry.

Seeing Henry's smile made Carlos feel giddy inside. He forgot how Henry made him feel. Carlos always felt safe and cared for when he dated him.

The bingo game was wrapping up, and they were going to set the floor up for dancing and the second part of the evening. The bar backs quickly removed the tables and decorations and cleaned the stage for the night's drag queens.

In all this time he spent with Henry at the bar, he hadn't stopped to think about the case.

"I don't want you to feel alone. Losing a parent is tough."

"I know you're there for me, CJ. I appreciate it. I've been sitting looking at all these papers on my father's desk about funeral arrangements, burial plots, and will readings, and I haven't had the stomach to read through them. I've got to do it soon because the funeral home has already called me twice and asked me to come down, but I told him I hadn't arrived in town yet. It's just too much. Jesus, I hate to vent."

Henry's voice trailed off. Carlos placed his hand on Henry's shoulder.

"I don't mind your venting. Everyone needs an outlet. Even you. Look, I know it's a lot with all the arrangements, and if you want, I can help you. When my aunt passed away two years ago, I was the one that handled everything: the funeral, burial, and even the will reading. All of it. When are you supposed to meet with the funeral director?"

"Tomorrow afternoon. I can't postpone it anymore."

People made a rush for the bar, as it was nearing one thirty. The lights in their section turned on slowly.

"Perfect, I've got some business in the morning, and when I'm done with it, I'll head over to your place after noon?"

"You're okay with helping me? You didn't even know my father."

"I didn't know your father well, but he was always helping the station with donations, and not to mention, he coached our softball league. He seemed like someone with his heart in the right place. Plus, I want to help you."

They finished the drinks they had and closed their tabs. By that time Valerie Paris and Betty Crocker finished their sets, the bar backs had cleared the stage for dancing. The lights of the bar dimmed, and black lights brought out the smiles on everyone at the bar.

Dan's seemed to morph from a gay dive bar to a seedy anything-goes club. Pairs of men headed off the dark back corners of the bar and resisted temptation no more. The music got louder, and the bass intensified. Carlos could substitute the beats of the song for his heart. Henry's eyes glanced over the glasses he'd emptied, then back to Carlos, where he could not take his eyes off him.

Carlos squeezed himself closer to Henry, wrapped his leg around Henry's and gave him an unexpected kiss on the mouth. Henry's eyes widened; the kiss was obviously unexpected but not unwanted. They locked lips for what seemed like minutes, but as the song changed in the background, they released the kiss and grabbed their stuff. Carlos led him out to the front entrance. He held his hand the entire way, and when outside, the pounding in their eyes stopped.

"I don't know what to say. I mean, that was nice."

"It was for me, too."

Carlos walked over to his car, and Henry followed. He clicked open his car and opened the driver's side door. He turned around to face Henry.

"I'm glad I got you out of the house for at least one night. I hope you feel better. I'll see you tomorrow."

"Yeah, of course."

Before getting into his car, Carlos could see Henry lingering and the wheels in his head were going into overdrive.

"Was there something else, Henry?"

"Um, well, I just thought it was kind of early still, you know."

Carlos' date reflexes were way off, and couldn't really tell if Henry was asking him to go home with him until the disappointed look appeared on his face.

"Oh, Henry, I can't stay out tonight. I've got to meet with

the medical examiner tomorrow before my shift starts at six. Another night?"

"Sure, no problem."

Carlos entered the car and sat down, rolling down his window and pulled Henry's face closer to his for another kiss. It wasn't as long as the one inside the bar, but none the less felt as colourful. Carlos couldn't figure out if it was the drinks or his emotions finally releasing.

Whatever the reason, it made him feel things he thought were long dead. Carlos zoomed out of the parking lot while he watched Henry shrink in his rearview mirror, but not in his heart.

9

Carlos woke up staring at his phone's alarm flashing 5:56 a.m., beeping its annoying shrill like it did almost every day, signalling it was time for a shower. Carlos' house was always quiet in the early morning hours. His brother David was still asleep from working the late shift at Benny's.

Carlos was glad about the job, but he could tell David wasn't all that excited about it. David hated to cook. Every time he talked about going to work, he substituted the word hell for work. David hated dealing with people. Actually, David hated pretty much everything and complained to Carlos daily.

After finishing his shower and getting dressed, Carlos stopped for a moment in front of David's open door. All was quiet except for Mr. Hamster, who was probably asking for food, wheeling away furiously. David was asleep in his work clothes and with one shoe still on.

His room was the polar opposite of how Carlos kept the house. David had two piles of clothes, which he called "the dirty stuff" and the "still-good-enough-to-wear stuff." His room reeked of body spray and B.O.

Unlike Carlos, David was a heavy sleeper and never woke up earlier than noon. He had that kind of lifestyle. The two of them hadn't been close growing up. After their sister died, being the only siblings left, it was no wonder they gravitated toward each other and had grown close. Their parents moved out of Valley City a decade earlier and gone to New Mexico—in part to retire, mostly to escape the memories. They sold the family home, and just like that, David found himself homeless.

Carlos just finished the academy and bought his first house, which he opened up to David, giving him a longer than expected temporary home which he hadn't left since. His mom used to send weekly texts asking Carlos to watch over David because he always had a hard time finding a job.

There was a part of Carlos that wished his parents didn't move away. At least David would have had a place to go to when things got tough. Their parents told everyone they were moving out west to retire and follow their dreams in a "steal of a deal" newly purchased home. It was more likely they couldn't bear to be around anyone or anything that reminded them of their daughter's death. Carlos didn't blame them for the move. After they left, the weight of the family shifted to him like an elephant cracking his back.

Sometimes, David's room was the only place where Carlos saw tiny little specks of dust floating and moving carelessly through the air. Carlos figured it was all the dirt and dust lingering around. When the sun was coming through the windows at a certain angle, the dust specks would shine and shimmer like bright pieces of floating crystals. With a wisp of air, they would go high and then slowly descend onto the ground, further from where they had started, but still in the same shape.

Those specks reminded Carlos of how David's life was until now. Moving from job to job, barely making enough money to cover his own food and never really making anything out of himself. He wondered how someone would be content just floating through the ether, never really gaining traction. Some people found that kind of lifestyle appealing, the spontaneity of it all. Carlos enjoyed routine and predictability. He didn't like to be surprised. That was the major difference between them.

One craved change, and one didn't.

Before David woke up, Carlos grabbed his keys from the wall and, just as he was about to close the front door, stopped suddenly, remembering to feed Mr. Hamster. Tossing a few pebbles his way, he smiled at him and silently left.

Outside, he found the morning fog remained ankle deep, almost creating a pathway to his car. As his feet passed the fog, swirls of cloud followed in his wake. He imagined it was like walking in a cloud. Before he entered his car, his phone beeped. It was a calendar notification to meet with the medical examiner. He replaced the phone in his pocket and headed to the station.

The morgue. According to the dictionary, it goes: "A place where bodies are kept, especially to be identified or claimed." A very clinical definition for a very clinical word. A place where bodies are claimed.

Seeing stacks and stacks of bodies was the part of visiting the medical examiner Carlos hated. The thought that dead bodies were mere inches away from him made his skin itch. The only thing separating him from them was a piece of metal. He hated going down there because it reminded him of his sister.

After she died, his parents were so crazed with emotion that they asked Carlos to take them to the morgue. He went along because he didn't want his parents to face it alone. Because of the visit, Carlos never got the image of his sister on the medical examiner's table out of his mind. He never went downstairs unless he absolutely needed to. He needed to find out more about what happened to Mr. Morelo and help Henry out.

Even the steps clacked a thin hollow unpleasant sound as he stepped down to the basement. The descent into the basement slapped Carlos in the face with its pungent and burning smell. The lights brightened to almost a glaring blindness as he entered the double flapped doors, where he found Dr. Zuniga, the medical examiner, wearing his typical blue scrubs, latex gloves, and protective face guard.

His old-time moustache poked out of his face mask, making for an odd picture. For someone with so much facial hair, Carlos found it odd he was bald. Carlos stopped at one of the unused examination tables and tapped the table a few times to grab his attention.

Dr. Zuniga's face went from somber to energetic.

"Detective Alvarado, good you're here. Thank you for being so prompt."

Dr. Zuniga motioned for him to meet him at an adjoining table, disappearing behind some curtains toward the back of the room. The morgue was bright and seemed impeccably hygienic. Every metal surface effortlessly shines, and the examining tables were neatly aligned, providing exactly three feet of space between workspaces. Various tubes lined the walls. Carlos was unaware of their purpose. He didn't want to know. From behind the curtain, Dr. Zuniga wheeled out Mr. Morelo and presented him to Carlos.

"Here we are."

Dr. Zuniga uncovered Mr. Morelo. He was losing his colour and almost looked peaceful in his slumber. A white sheet covered up to his shoulder, and his hair seemed to be combed and greased back. Mr. Morelo had dark, sagging eyes bulging from his face. He had a neatly trimmed moustache and goatee, with large thick sideburns down to his cheekbones. There was a dark mole that dominated his right cheek.

Carlos peered at him and thought of this man raising Henry and how their relationship might have been. Henry mentioned nothing about how his life had been growing up. Even when they dated in high school, they always spent time at his house and never Henry's.

Although, one evening, when Carlos' parents would not be home, they insisted Carlos and Henry spend time at Henry's home. Carlos' parents were deeply Christian and strictly believed children were not allowed home alone without supervision.

They insisted they spend the evening at Henry's place. Carlos saw the fear in Henry's eyes. He wasn't sure what Henry feared, but he knew something was on his mind and went along with it. When they arrived outside his home, Henry stopped him from exiting the car.

"CJ, my parents are very old school. They are super traditional, and even though they know that I'm gay and we are dating, they still aren't used to it. They refer to you as my friend. It really pisses me off, and then there's my sister. She's ten years older than me, and she still lives at home and is always up in my business. I just really can't wait to get out there and go to school at UNT when we graduate and be on our own. We won't have to worry about all this mess."

"Just take a second and breathe. Here, give me your hand."

Carlos held his hand and placed it against his chest.

"I want you to close your eyes and feel our hands moving

up and down as I breathe. Feel for my heartbeat. Try to imagine my heart beating against your hand and block out all that nasty noise."

Henry's face muscles seemed to relax, and his breathing slowed.

"You always know how to chill me out. I'm such a mess, and you balance me out."

Henry bent over the console to kiss Carlos. Their lips met and danced against each other's faces for a few moments before Henry got the courage to exit the car.

"Alright, I think I'm ready. Let's go."

Henry walked the length of the sidewalk and opened his front door.

Inside, they were greeted by Henry's parents, who said the minimalist of hellos and introductions before retreating to their business. Henry's father sat at their kitchen table, fiddling with some graph paper and scissors. He had piles of newspapers and stacks of pens. He arranged his paper, cutting and stapling with unexpected speed for someone his age.

It reminded Carlos of how a kindergartener looked the first time they were handed scissors and were introduced to construction paper. The determination and joy that came from his eyes were uncommon. It made Carlos envious that Mr. Morelo had something good in his life.

Mrs. Morelo attached herself to the TV, watching some Mexican soap opera. She was wearing what could only be described as a muumuu and slippers. Crosses adorned the walls of his parents' room, along with a dresser dedicated to a shrine of various candles. Carlos smelt the burning wicks of jasmine and musk incense in the room.

They entered the hallway and found their way to Henry's small and well-kept room. Cracked cement, supposed to be the foundation of the house, littered the floor in Henry's small and well-kept room instead of tile or carpet. Henry explained their house suffered damage during last year's flood, and the government money didn't meet his father's expectations. The house was a work in progress.

None of it mattered to Carlos. What he remembered about that day was spending time with Henry watching episodes of *The Office* and *How I Met Your Mother* from his DVD collection. That was the one thing that Henry was most proud of. He had a bit of everything. Sometimes he would pull out his collection and declare it "Random Show Tuesday."

Whatever he picked out, we would be forced to watch in its entirety, whether it was at his house or Carlos'. Sometimes they got lucky, and sometimes they didn't. Regardless, it was more time that Carlos could spend with Henry.

Carlos also remembered it as the first time they ever had sex. The one thing about Henry's parents it was they were so embarrassed about Henry being gay, they never checked in on him for fear of what they might see if they entered. This gave them the green light to explore each other. Carlos paused for a moment to remember their first time.

As they both slowly and methodically drew their clothes off, he ran his hands along Henry's lower back, just above his butt. Carlos remembered the smoothness of his rounded cheeks. Their skin against each other caused Carlos's heart to almost jump out of his chest. The raciness of it made him physically jitter, almost bumping his head against Henry's chin. Henry seemed to communicate what he wanted with a simple smile and an invitation to join him under the covers.

Carlos sensed the heat emanating from Henry while they were lying next to each other naked, their chests pressed together and their lips locked. He moaned and whimpered as if being touched for the first time. Carlos knew it hadn't been his first nor his own, but it still felt special between them. Theirs was an urge he never felt before. As Carlos rolled Henry over and felt his eagerness enter Henry, all he heard was a gasp and sigh. Carlos placed his chin on Henry's shoulder and twisted Henry's back so he could see and hear him. The whites of Henry's eyes were all Carlos saw. He knew his body and mind were somewhere on the other side of erotica. Even afterward, as the rawness and bliss of it wore off, Carlos couldn't stop smiling. It was a giddiness that didn't seem to want to dissipate.

THE BUZZING AND CRACKLING OF THE BRIGHT overhead lights killed his train of thought. Carlos only wondered what kind of relationship Henry and his father had. He pondered whether he and his father ever engaged in discussions about life, death, or even the future. His questions would go unanswered for now, as he needed to ask Dr. Zuniga some questions. Carlos noticed that Mr. Morelo had the same nose as Henry's. It dominated his facial structure and had a slightly rounded bend pointing down.

"Doc, can you tell me what you've learned thus far? Anything out of the ordinary," Carlos said, as he opened his notebook to the next clean page.

"As expected, I found brodifacoum in his system. There were trace amounts that showed he was ingesting it for approximately two and a half weeks. It levelled out at around twenty to twenty-five milligrams. But that isn't what killed him. It was a combination of two things. According to Mr. Morelo's medical records, he was being treated for a mild heart attack that he had several months ago. He was taking one hundred milligrams of Toprol twice a day. It's a beta blocker that is given to patients after they've suffered a heart attack. The drug itself should be present in the bloodstream for approximately four to six hours after its last dose. We couldn't find any trace of it in his system."

"He stopped taking his meds, so?"

"That's not the entire story. What we found in his system concerns me. We found high levels of methamphetamine."

"Are you telling me Mr. Morelo was a meth head? I just don't buy it."

"I'm not suggesting anything like that. I ran the test three times because certain heart medications often provide false positives for methamphetamines, but since we couldn't locate the Toprol in his system, the false positive was ruled out. As far as how he ingested the methamphetamine, that's a mystery. There wasn't any lung or oral damage that is usually associated with the drug. What I know for certain is that the combination of methamphetamine and the absence of his heart medicine caused his cardiac arrest."

"I just can't see the man using drugs. Is there any other way for the drug to have gotten into his system, secondhand smoke or something?"

"Detective, not at these levels. They are too high to be something someone casually inhaled as a passerby. The concentration of the drug tells me he must have ingested it approximately three to four days prior to his death."

"That gives me a window to work with, Doc. Anything else that you might think I'd find helpful?"

"Those were the only anomalies. Besides that, he was in good health, and according to his medical doctor, he was on his way to making a full recovery from his previous heart attack."

"Thanks, Doc. I'll let you get back to work. Thanks for the update."

Carlos looked at Mr. Morelo one more time. His eyes had lost the fire he once seen in them back when Carlos and Henry were in high school. He had the same withdrawn and distant eyes his sister had all those years ago.

Uncertain how to approach Henry, he worried about sharing his findings. He didn't want their meeting later to be discoloured by this news. He needed to decide to tell him before or after.

Either way, it was a conversation he wasn't looking forward to having.

10

With only twenty dollars left to his name, Benny's fired David. Finding he couldn't go to Mr. Morelo anymore for extra cash, he took the brief trip to Treasure Hills and visited Ruben, who didn't live far from his place of business.

His house stood at a cul-de-sac near the county club. White brick covered the entire house, which stood two stories high. It was a well-manicured lawn and Mexican Blue Palm trees lined its entrance. The leaves of the palm trees fanned out ten to twenty feet across, obscuring the view from outside and providing privacy. In the sun, it almost doubled in its brightness. Despite having a house twice the size of his neighbours, Ruben lived alone.

It was one thing David enjoyed about coming over to his place. There was no one to bother them or interrupt them. What came along with the privacy was another matter entirely. Ruben and David were having an off-and-on fling for several months now. Ever since David's connection for meth dried up, he was going to Ruben for re-ups. A guy from work had tipped him off to Ruben's shop as a place where he could score. Having no choice, he made the trip and had hoped he would not get screwed over.

Thinking back now, David was taking a risk going to a stranger's place of business, asking for drugs and hoping it would all go well. Then again, that's what drugs will do to you. Throw all common sense out the window.

WHEN DAVID ARRIVED AT RUBEN'S SHOP, IT WAS closed, and no one was around. David almost left, but the front door clicked open. Inside, the lights were off, and sounds seemed to come from the back room. Knocking on the door that was labeled EMPLOYEES ONLY, a soft voice offered entrance.

The room was dark except for a small lamp and an overhead black light, which gave the room a purple hue. It exaggerated the whites in the room. Ruben was sitting in one of the few chairs in the room and offered David the other one.

He had a smile on his face reaching almost ear to ear and had a thin build and seemed kind of scrawny, making him appear younger than he was. A thinning head of hair gave away his age. The man had no facial or body hair from David's vantage point.

David immediately noticed a purple school box on the table with its lid open. Inside, he saw his familiar old friends, baggies of crystal, an oiler, and a torch. David's eyes were so laser-focused on them, he almost forgot about Ruben.

"Excuse me, young man, I'm over here."

"Sorry, sorry, it's just I've never seen that much crystal before. It's gotta be like more than a g, right?" Ruben chuckled.

"In fact, you're looking at an eight-ball."

"Fuck, an eight-ball! That must be expensive. All I can afford is twenties."

David pulled his folded-up twenty out of his pocket and placed it on the table.

Ruben slid the bill back to David.

"As a businessman, I always pride myself on great customer service. The first time is on me. So put your money away."

"What's the catch? There's always a catch."

"No catch. Just have fun and relax. We can have a good time."

Ruben grabbed his oiler and placed the biggest rock David had ever seen go in. Ruben held the pipe in David's mouth and lit it for him, instructing when to inhale and when to stop. David blew out the largest billow of smoke he ever made, making his head spin in the way that made it all much better.

Ruben's Cheshire smile grew even further and from that point on, David never looked back and should have realized Ruben's controlling nature, but was too high to notice.

***

Because of their off-and-on relationship, it sometimes made it hard for them to party together. Ruben was always on the kinkier side of things, and when David smoked, it was hard for him to say no. David often found himself in situations he normally wouldn't put himself in.

Ruben knew David well and knew exactly how to handle him when he smoked. As the night went on and more people arrived, David often found himself in a vulnerable position, open to whatever the group desired. Ruben liked to watch as strangers took advantage of David and had their way with him. Usually waiting till the end of the night for his turn at David. Ruben loved being last.

It was for this reason David had second thoughts about going to Ruben's. If he didn't, he wouldn't be able to smoke. The crystal always won the argument, and he knocked on Ruben's door, anyway. Ruben answered, and inside, he could already hear porn on the TV. Ruben was already drinking and had the lights to a minimum.

"Glad you came, babe. I was wondering if you were going to head over tonight."

"I wasn't going to, but you know how it goes."

"I do."

Ruben retrieved his oiler and handed it to David.

Regrettably, he took a long, well developed hit out of the oiler and held it in for as long as he could. His eyes went from bright and defined to mellow and dark. David's face tickled with change as the effects of the crystal coursed through his blood. The muscles on his face relaxed, his brow lowered, and the exasperation of relief of tension exited his body.

In an instant, he forgot about all the things that were bothering him. There were no more thoughts of being fired from his job or worrying about money. As long as he was with Ruben, Ruben would take care of him. Sometimes these benders lasted days and upwards of a week. It all depended on how badly David didn't want to face the world that day.

Releasing the smoke from his lungs, he rushed air in. Like clockwork, after taking the first hit and feeling the small ember grow in his stomach, his shirt and shoes came right off. David remained this way for the rest of the evening. Crystal always made him feel like disrobing, but he needed to be careful. Taking off all his clothes was an unspoken statement that he was ready to fuck, and that wasn't the case. David just wanted to forget the world, forget about Pops.

When they took Pops away, it became too much for him because Pops had become a father figure to him. Like David's father, who simply wanted nothing to do with him and left the state with his mother, he once again found himself alone, with no parental support. It was much easier to not deal with it than to deal with it. In his crystal-filled haze, he began thinking about Pops and how he always threw him a bone or an odd job when he was low on cash.

Some people found it weird that David called Mr. Morelo "Pops" when he had a father of his own. Truth be told, David and his father never saw eye-to-eye. David's father always seemed to favour his older brother Carlos, who was always the exemplary child, and David ended up with scraps.

When Carlos graduated high school and left David behind, he thought it was his chance to have his father's attention. That wasn't the case. His father was always comparing David to Carlos and how David was lagging and not meeting or exceeding the example that Carlos had set forth.

If Carlos got an A, David needed an A+.

It never ended.

When David wanted to save money for a car, his father forbade him from having a car because he hadn't passed his driver's test on the first try, like Carlos. Even when he wanted to learn how to play the piano, his father told him no again. There wasn't enough money, his father would say, yet his brother always seemed to get new clothes every school year.

David never understood why his father always preferred Carlos to him, but it didn't matter in the end. When his parents moved to New Mexico, he finally felt as if he could live freely and without their disapproving eyes.

One day after David was working at Benny's for a while, Mr. Morelo came in and sat in the same booth he always did, ordering the same thing he did every time: decaf coffee with nondairy creamer and Splenda, reading the newspaper and writing in a tiny notebook always before leaving.

On the first day, after David took his order, he noticed that

Mr. Morelo had mowed grass covering the bottoms of his pants. Enthralled by what he did, David didn't want to bother him, but he didn't want to let an opportunity pass him by.

"Looks like you just came in from mowing your lawn, huh?"

"What? Oh."

Mr. Morelo looked at his pants.

"Si, did the lawn today, and it took me forever. The lawn sucks, but I'm the only one who can do it, so no point in complaining," said Santos.

David had an idea.

"You know, my father used to own a landscaping business, and I have experience in a lot of the equipment. If you ever need someone to do your yard, I could help you out. I wouldn't charge much. I just want to make some extra cash. Tips aren't good here and besides; he left all his equipment here with me."

David pointed to the other customers while pointing to his elbow. "You know, codo, cheap right?"

Santos nodded in agreement. There was a flurry of other servers all with smiles and thick padded aprons, assumably with cash. David's was empty.

"Mijo, I couldn't pay you much. I'm on a fixed income and on a budget. I normally do it myself, but lately I just haven't been in the mood. It's been tough."

David kneeled at the table before speaking. "Is everything alright sir? I mean, you look a little sad. Can't your kids help you mow the lawn or help around the house? I hope I'm not intruding."

"No, my kids are all grown up and don't live with me. They all moved away outside of state, so it's just me," said Santos, as he took a beat. "Even if they were here, I doubt they would help. We don't get along too well, plus my health hasn't been too good lately."

"Gosh, that sucks. Dang, sir. I can relate. My brother is always on my ass and my parents left a long time ago to retire, so there's no help there. I feel ya," said David.

Santos thought about it for a moment.

"But if you really need the extra cash, I'm sure I can find some extra way to help you. But you do a good job."

"Of course. My father taught me. I can do it."

"Then okay. You can come over to my house next week, and I'll show you what I need done. I'll write my number here on the check, and you can call me on Friday."

The sun bled into the room, causing shadows to appear on most of the tables. A mass of people began exiting the restaurant, all attempting to pay, causing a buildup at the cashier stand. David's section suddenly thinned into a ghost town.

"You got it, Pops."

David realized he had called him Pops.

"Pops?"

Mr. Morelo looked quizzical.

"Oh, I'm sorry. I didn't mean nothing by it."

David slouched as he pondered his choice of words.

"Mijo, it's okay. Pops is kind of nice."

Mr. Morelo left the table, but not before leaving a twenty-dollar tip on the table and snaking all the extra sugars into his pocket. After that, "Pops" it was.

***

The following Friday afternoon, David showed up at Mr. Morelo's house right on time. As he showed David around the outside of the house, David's phone kept beeping. So much, in fact, that Mr. Morelo noticed.

"David, if there is someplace you need to be, we can do this another time. I don't want to keep you from stuff."

"No, no, Pops. We're good. It's nothing."

A few hours into working on the lawn, Ruben kept trying to reach David. It was Friday evening, and he must have just gotten done closing the shop and wanted to see David. They usually partied on weekends and made three days blur into one. David was sure Ruben would find it strange he wasn't picking up his phone, but he placed the phone on silent anyway and put the thought out of his head and focused on Mr. Morelo.

Pops took David to the backyard, where it was more bush than yard. A concrete sidewalk divided it, broken in two by the root of a tree. It almost made his backyard look like it had its own mini hill. Beyond the back gate, David saw the nearby canal. Some tall shrubs that lined the bank of the canal mostly hid it. The shrubs stuck out above the bank and guarded it like a wall around a castle. In between the branches, you could see glimpses of the water moving at a steady pace. Some branches had brown points on the end of them with what looked like white feathers dangling by a thread. When the breeze hit the trees, flurries of white threads covered the landscape. It almost looked like it was snowing.

Mr. Morelo invited him inside for something to drink after his task. Mr. Morelo walked David to the living room, where he sat down on the only couch in the room. There was only a large mirror on one end and a small dresser displaying a set of pictures on Mr. Morelo's bare walls.

As David waited for Mr. Morelo to grab him something to drink, he walked over to the dresser. There were two pictures on display, one of himself and what David assumed was his wife, and the other was of three children. David picked up the photo of the children and turned it around. The label on the last family portrait read Henry, Santos Jr., and Rose. What an odd name for a picture, David thought. Mr. Morelo exited the kitchen with drinks in hand.

"I hope you like agua de Jamaica."

"I do. I was looking at your pictures. Is that your family? What happened to them? I mean, did they move out of town or—"

Mr. Morelo grabbed the photos and placed them inside a drawer before David finished his sentence, slamming the dresser closed and turning away from David. David's eyes sunk down knowing he had made a mistake and asked too much, then placed a hand on Mr. Morelo's shoulder.

David didn't know the words to say so instead he stayed silent, and his hand placement became a hug which Santos did not object to. The embrace lasted several seconds before David spoke up.

"I'm sorry. I don't even know why I asked you that," David said as he sipped his drink.

"You know, I have a brother who's only two years older than me. He's a cop. I mean a detective. We really don't get along."

"Un detective, eh? Que bueno. I'm sure your parents are proud of him."

"They are. A little too much, if you ask me. They always compare me to him. They want me to have his life and follow in his footsteps. I don't want to go to college like him. I just want to be left alone to figure out what it is I want to do. I don't even know what that is anymore."

"David, sometimes the best way to find your way is to lose your way. My father used to tell me that all the time. I never knew what he meant exactly, but I know when you find what makes you happy, you'll know."

Mr. Morelo placed a hand on David's shoulder.

"That's easy for you to say. I have no clue what makes me happy. My brother tells me every day I need to find a career or go to school. I live in his house rent-free, and I guess that's his way of caring for me. It really sucks. I just wish I could find something other than Benny's. It blows there."

"I'm sure you will find it someday. Just keep an open mind."

By now, David's energy was dropping, and the itching on the left palm of his hand was undeniable and needed to hit the oiler before he mowed Mr. Morelo's lawn. So, he asked permission to use the bathroom, and Morelo pointed him in the direction. David walked past a small hallway where two bedrooms were located. The shut doors prevented him from seeing inside the bedrooms.

In the bathroom, he found it sparsely decorated. Everything was in the colour green, even the toilet seat. Looking around the room for a bathroom vent, he found one in the ceiling, flipping the switch on, causing a loud buzzing sound to come on. This was exactly what David needed. The noise to cover the sounds of his lighter, flicking on and off while he hit the oiler.

Every subsequent hit, he blew the smoke toward the toilet bowl and flushed. David wasn't sure if it did anything, but it was a habit he had always had. After he was done, the blood returned to his hands and feet, and he could feel the burning sensation inside his lungs.

Opening the medicine cabinet, he found many typical things like Tylenol, allergy medicine and others in pill bottles he didn't recognize. In the first fleeting moments of being high, sometimes it would cause David to be a major snooper into other people's things. Since nothing seemed of value, he simply ignored the strange container in the back of the cabinet that was labeled d-Con. Before heading back out, he glanced at the mirror one last time now that he was back to feeling normal.

After he finished mowing the lawn, he sat on the back porch. Mr. Morelo left him a giant-sized bottle of water, dripping with condensation, ready for him. After he turned the machine off, the noises of the night took over. Sounds of frogs and crickets ruled the airwaves. Mr. Morelo came around the corner, having just gotten off the phone. The sun was setting, and the light was reflecting off the waters of the canal. His body ached after the work of the evening, but even more so since his body was now sweating out the drugs. The lack of sleep was catching up to him.

David took a long, well-deserved chug of water. He seemed like he would not stop for a breath of air, but at the last second, he relented. The bottle of water was nearly empty. David kept staring at the banks of the canal and wondered what was in its depth, hearing splashes of water from time to time.

"I wonder if there's any fish in the canal, you think?"

"You know, I don't know. I never been fishing there, probably only alligator, gar or catfish. You fish?"

David finished the rest of his water.

"Naw, not really. I haven't been since I was younger. My dad used to take me when I was in elementary."

David shrugged his shoulders.

"I remember it being fun, though. It was the one thing that my dad and I did alone. He had never invited my brother. I asked him one time how come, and he just told me that Carlos wasn't big on the outdoors. It didn't really matter, anyway. I had just been happy to do anything alone with my dad."

David sensed the breeze off the canal wash over him. The distinct aroma of fish wafted up his nose as the cicadas rang in the distance.

"My dad would take me down the road from where we lived to the city lake near the library. There, we would sit in our folding chairs with our fishing poles, waiting for bites. Honestly, I don't remember catching any fish. I just remember my dad telling me stories about when his father had taken him fishing and how much he loved it. The sad thing is that after a while, we just stopped going. I can't even remember why. I remember on the day of our last trip out to the lake; my parents had this huge fight in the kitchen."

As he remembered the fight, his shoulders tensed and the fear that had subsided brimmed back to the surface.

"Carlos and I were in our bedroom watching TV when, out of nowhere, we heard glass break and loud thumping noises from the kitchen. I wanted to go out and see what was happening, but Carlos wouldn't let me. He said that because he was the older brother, it was his job to find out and protect me. So, I waited in the room while he went to look."

The details have always remained fuzzy when he tried to remember it before, but telling Mr. Morelo, the fog lifted, and it just flowed out of him.

"When he came back, Carlos seemed angry and had his hands in fists and kept pacing the room and wouldn't tell me what had happened. I heard doors open and shut in my parents' room, and that was it. It was quiet for the rest of the evening. Carlos never exactly told me what he saw, but whatever it was, he seemed like a different person after that."

Santos's brow fell, and he grabbed David's hand. The bug zapper automatically turning on at sunset, buzzed as it caught an unsuspecting fly.

"My god, mijo. That's terrible. I really don't talk much to people anymore since everyone moved out of the house. It's just me. I almost forgot how it felt to talk to anyone for more than a few minutes. It sounds like you have been through a lot, and I want you to know that if you ever want to share anything else with me, I can be a good listener. It helps."

Mr. Morelo grabbed the gold bracelet on his left wrist and spun it. It had three pieces of ivory-coloured orbs hanging from it. A silver-tinted string connected the orbs to each other. He rubbed his fingers on each orb and let out a sigh.

"Pops, I'm down too if you wanna ever talk about anything. I can have a good ear too. I guess that's why I don't get along with my dad much or even talk to him. It just got weird after that, and it never felt the same again. Something just felt off, and then they just ran away to New Mexico. They said it was to retire near the mountains, but it sounds like bullshit to me. Doesn't matter anymore. I'm over it now. Crazy how seeing that canal down there reminded me of all that shit."

"Memory is funny like that."

"Pops, I see you messing with that bracelet all the time. Is it special or something?"

"This thing? I had this for a long time. Mi esposa, my wife got it for me after we had our last child Henry, you see here the three little bolas de ivory?"

"You mean those orb looking things?"

"Si, si, those. My wife said she got it from some curandera who blessed it with yerbabuena (mint) and rue, so our children would be prosperous. I carry it to remind me that somewhere out there the kids I hope are doing ok."

"Pops, I didn't know you believed in curanderas and all that."

"Well, I don't know David. You know never know."

It was the same thing every time David came over to work on Mr. Morelo's lawn or to help him with some odd job. The work lasted an hour, and then they spent hours talking about all sorts of stuff.

It was no wonder David called Santos "Pops" who had practically grown into another father figure. They both enjoyed each other's company.

After Pops died, David felt something inside of him he hadn't felt in a long time, a sensation reminiscent of what it was like sitting in his childhood room alone, waiting for his brother Carlos to come back and tell him what happened. The sensation hit him as if the room had sucked out all the air and the ceiling was crushing him.

The seconds of silence seemed to drag on and felt like glacial hours instead of seconds. Sitting alone caused him to come up with many crazy ideas about what could happen outside his room. With no answer in sight, waiting was the worst.

Just like that, he seemed so disconnected. David felt like he lost more than a friend and employer in Mr. Morelo. He lost Pops, and it hurt more than words would convey. It was the hurt which drove David to Ruben's. The weight became too much. The one person who normally would hear him out when shit had gone bad was gone.

11

Henry pulled up to the Valley Memorial Funeral Home, wondering why his father choose this place above all others. It seemed too fancy for someone like his father. The long driveway from the street entrance almost seemed too grand for a funeral home. Palm trees swaying in the wind lined it. Red caliche rocks sat on the bed of the trees where smaller bushes surrounded the base of the trees.

To each side, a delicate lawn spread across what seemed like several acres. The cemetery lay beside the lawn and off to the back. Several gates and eight-foot-tall fences guarded it. Inside were even more well-kept lawns, with burial plots running the entire length of Treasure Hills boulevard. Its winding hills sloped down and up, with mesquite trees dotting the landscape.

The funeral home itself was beige brick with orange and brown rust-colored caliche stones. It had great ten-foot opulent windows that showcased the selling floor portion of the funeral home. Lines and lines of caskets of all different sizes and shapes filled the room. Henry had never seen such a funeral home display that kind of stature. It almost seemed

89

like an opulent residence and less like a funeral home. The parking lot was empty except for a few cars. Henry looked down at his phone and found he had arrived early, and Carlos was nowhere in sight.

Henry entered the funeral home anyway. Through the large brown varnished door, he encountered an old-fashioned environment. White and blue wallpaper covered every single inch of the walls, while gold-framed mirrors hung on the side of the walls, facing each other and creating an optical illusion that made the room seem bigger.

There had been this story that Henry's grandmother had shared with him the last time she came to visit before she passed away. She said when mirrors face each other it causes the energy in the room to be in constant flux and recycle into each other over and over. This would cause anyone near it to be off balance and almost amplify your worries and uncertainty. She believed your soul could get stuck in this infinite loop, leading to it being forever lost. Henry's grandmother had always been the superstitious type and the kind that kept candles lit to ward off evil spirits.

His own mother or father had passed none of this down to Henry. Ghosts and spirits were not something he thought about. When he entered the funeral home and saw the mirrors, he wondered why the funeral home would arrange such a setup where death is constant. If Henry had believed in ghosts and spirits, he would have thought that this funeral home would have a long rotating cast of visitors that kept the energy of grieving people in constant flux. If Henry had believed in that, but he didn't. Still, it made him a little nauseous when peering into the mirrors.

In between the mirrors stood a grand staircase with red velvet-lined steps that led to the visitors' balcony. The bottom floor was mainly for the funeral home business and wasn't open to the public. Under the stairs, Henry could hear compressor-like sounds starting and stopping while a man shouted under the noise. Not being able to make out what was being said, but Henry could tell it didn't sound like he was having a good time. Before anyone appeared out from under the stairs, he headed up the stairs to the balcony. Up top, he found himself surrounded by redder velvet-coloured chairs, carpets, and even fireplace trims. A sign-in sheet stood near the only door upstairs, figuring he should write his name down and take a seat.

The quietness of the room reminded him of a church even though Henry hadn't been to church since his mother had forced him to attend his catholic confirmation. Even as a child, Henry had never seen much value in going to church. His mother insisted every time they attend church, but he fought her every time. In the end, he made a deal with her to only attend church until he completed his confirmation.

According to the church, confirmation is when an individual confers the holy spirit into their life and does so when they can understand that commitment. For Henry, it meant something different; it was his opportunity to get his mother off his back about going to church. On the day of the confirmation, Henry had put on his best church suit and black loafers; combing his hair back and slicking it still with the hair gel. At the church, during the ceremony, he could see his mother in the front pews watching him intently.

After the bishop read his name aloud and asked if he was ready to accept the holy spirit into his life completely and wholly, Henry nodded and recited his name and commitment with a smile on his face. After doing so, his mother clapped in approval and wiped away her tears from her face. Henry had never seen his mother cry.

Henry had planned after the ceremony to tell his mother that she had gotten what she wanted, and now he was done, quitting the church and stepping away from God. Henry had wanted to find his own way. After seeing her cry and how happy she had been over such a simple thing, though, he changed his mind. In under eight months, he would be off to college, and he wouldn't need to worry about church anymore. Henry decided it was worth pretending a little longer if it kept his mother happy.

A man entered the room, interrupting his reverie. The man was wearing a dark gray suit with a matching tie and shoes. His bald spot was visible as he slicked his hair off to the side. He limped over to Henry and extended his hand.

"Good morning. My name is Raul Garza. This is my establishment. Do you have an appointment, Mr.?"

"Henry Morelo. I believe you left me a couple of messages."

Henry looked down at his watch and wondered where Carlos was because he really didn't want to be alone with Mr. Garza. Funeral arrangements were something he wouldn't know where to begin with. Mr. Garza led him into his office down the hall from the waiting room. Charitable awards and pictures of the business through its three-decade existence lined the walls.

"Of course, Mr. Morelo. Thank you for coming, and I am sincerely sorry for your loss. I heard your father was a well-liked man in town. A donation fund has already been started in his name. Will there be anyone else joining you or?"

"A donation fund? Someone started one. Who?"

Rudy reached for his phone and flipped a few screens before stopping.

"Looks like the Valley City Police Department and a private business named Treasure Hills Graphics. They donated a few thousand dollars each toward whatever its benefactor would see fit to use it for."

"And who's the benefactor?"

"They have listed you as his next of kin."

"That's bizarre. I'm grateful, but I guess I didn't know my father that well. I had no clue he had such close ties with the community. I mean, I knew he coached the charity softball team for the police force, but this seems crazy to me. And that local business. I think my father had ties with them."

"Consider it a blessing, then. We don't get those too much around here, so when we do, it's good to take the win, you know."

"Thank you, Mr. Garza. I appreciate it."

Henry felt a tap at his waist and turned around. Carlos had arrived.

"You finally showed up. I didn't even hear you come up the stairs."

"You can thank those red velvet steps. So plush."

Carlos extended his hand over to Rudy, who immediately focused on the gun at his hip.

"Good to meet you, Mr. Garza. I'm Detective Alvarado. I'm here for moral support and to help in any way I can."

"Good for you. We all could use some moral support during trying times like these. It's always hard to lose a parent. Why don't the both of you come into my office, and we can look at the package I've set up for Mr. Morelo? If you have questions, speak up. I don't mind."

The office's corner-facing window overlooked the adjacent cemetery and rolling hills for several blocks, admitting natural light. Soft jazz music was playing just loud enough that it wouldn't intrude into any conversation. The room itself carried a warm scent of cinnamon that Henry couldn't place its source from, that is until he saw the giant bowl of broken up cinnamon sticks behind Rudy. A lush garden grew near the cemetery, where groundskeepers harvested roses into baskets. His desk had a large computer monitor that swivelled between himself and the guest chairs in front of him. It made it easier for him to show his clients the options available. If it hadn't been for the low buzz of the music, the groundskeeper's machinery would have made the conversation difficult.

"So, my first question is a bit sensitive. I hope you don't mind. How close were you with your father?"

Henry tapped his thumbs together back and forth several times before speaking. Carlos's eyes leered down at Henry's hands. He had seen him do that before; always when he got nervous, so he scooted his chair over to be closer to Henry. The tapping stopped.

"My father and I haven't spoken in almost ten years. I honestly can't say we were close anymore."

"That's unfortunate, but understandable. The reason I ask is your father left a will and had specific instructions on how he would like his last wishes to be carried out."

Raul moused over a few tabs in the computer monitor until he got to Santos' will documents.

"Here we are, so it looks like your father has requested a traditional full-service funeral which comprises a viewing of the deceased here in the funeral home, a funeral service at our cemetery, the transportation, of course, and the actual burial itself. Did you view the documents I sent over via email?"

Henry sat in the chair fixated on the outside cemetery and its rolling hills going almost a full minute before Carlos stepped in and spoke.

"Mr. Garza, I was wondering how much something like that is going to cost. I don't know exactly Henry's finances, but I'm sure he would like to minimize the costs as much as he can. I am sure he just overlooked the documents in all the stress of planning."

"Of course, we offer varying packages to fit any budgetary needs. The minimal cost for what Mr. Morelo requested would run between six and eight thousand dollars."

Henry tapped his knee now on the red velvet floors. The plushness of the carpet muted any noise. Carlos took a second to place his hand on Henry's knee to reassure him. Henry's tapping lessened.

"That sounds about right. I handled my aunt's last wishes a few years ago, and it cost us seventy-five hundred dollars."

Carlos looked over at Henry.

"Henry, is that going to be fine? Is that manageable?"

Henry cleared his throat of the dryness.

"Mr. Garza, is there enough in the collection fund to cover that amount?"

Carlos scrunched his face. Since this was the first he was hearing of it.

"Yes, Mr. Morelo, you will end up with a surplus of over fifteen hundred dollars for any last-minute changes to his service. Now I have drafted an obituary notice that will run in the *Valley Morning Star* if you want to review it ahead of time."

Raul flipped his tabs and twisted his monitor, so it was visible to Henry and Carlos.

On the screen, Henry, for the first time in almost ten years, saw a picture of his father. His father was wearing a Dallas Cowboys cap and jersey. Henry noticed his father let his moustache and sideburns grow longer than he remembered. His eyes appeared sunken, and little specks of hair poked out the sides of the cap. There was no smile present, yet he didn't look angry. Henry realized that the next time he saw his father, it would be at the viewing, and he imagined he would look very different from his picture. Mr. Garza waited for Henry's response, but it never came.

"Mr. Garza, if you don't mind, would it be okay if he decided on the notice at another time?"

"I don't see why not. It needs to be completed before the middle of the week if you want to have the service this weekend."

Henry nodded.

"Mr. Morelo, the only other piece of business is the reading of the will. I am sure your father's attorney has been in contact with you. Your father left specific instructions for it. The only family member mentioned in the will was you, Mr. Morelo. There was no mention of any other family members. His wishes are for it to be read directly after the funeral service. We have a library on the other side of the building where you can have some privacy when the time comes."

"Thank you, Mr. Garza. You've given me a lot to think about. I will call you before the middle of the week to make any final arrangements if that's alright with you?"

Mr. Garza agreed and walked them out of his office and down the stairs toward the entranceway. On the opposite side of the stairs was the sales floor, where all the model caskets were on display. The room narrowed and showcased caskets on both sides of the room. Some were open, some were closed, some were made of wood, and others were made of metal, causing the room to have a sanitized smell to it.

Toward the middle of the room stood a sign that said, "Please look around. Our caskets are your caskets." Henry couldn't figure out if it was funny or literal. Either way, being around death and cemeteries had caused him to seize up. He just stood there, staring at the lines of caskets. His eyes darted between each one and caused his eyelids to twitch. His feet tapped the floor simultaneously.

Henry noticed Carlos watching him as he lost his balance. Maybe he had pushed himself too soon to come to the funeral home. Whatever the reason, he tried to put up a brave front for Carlos to not seem weak.

"Woah, woah, woah, Henry, are you alright?"

"I, I just need to get out of here. Can we leave, please?"

Carlos grabbed Henry's arm, and they strolled out the front door. The wind gushed over them, and a scent of roses wafted into their noses. Henry directed him to his car. Outside his car, he fumbled to find his keys in his pockets, stopping to take a deep breath and then open his car door. The air had become humid and made his car feel like an oven. With no other cars in sight, the only sounds heard were the palm trees whipping in the wind.

"Are you going to be okay to drive, Henry?"

"I just had a moment back there. I'm good now. I promise."

"Good. Look, I've got to get back to the station and follow up on some things, but why don't you call me tomorrow, and we'll see if we can meet up once I'm done with work?"

"Sounds fine."

"Can I ask you something, though?"

"Alright."

Henry rolled down the window. He started the engine and maxed his A/C.

"The funeral director mentioned a donation fund. Did he tell you who the funds came from?"

"Yeah, your police department and Treasure Hills Graphics, the same business you asked me about the other day."

"I'll have to look into it."

"You have said nothing about my father's death. Have you found anything out I should know about?"

Henry could tell by Carlos's averting eyes he had hoped to avoid this conversation, especially outside of the funeral home. It brought back flashbacks of him lying to protect his feelings and it was not something he wanted to repeat but until he was certain he would give Carlos the benefit of the doubt.

"I'm supposed to meet with the medical examiner later to get an update. How about when we meet tomorrow, I fill you in?"

Henry could have sworn that he had already met with the medical examiner, but perhaps he was wrong.

"Sure."

They hugged and were off in their own directions.

CARLOS KNEW HE TOLD HENRY A LIE, BUT HE STILL wasn't ready to tell him about what he knew. The connection between Ruben Delgado and Henry's father ran deeper than simply donating clothes, and Carlos needed more time to figure it out.

12

David sat in his room at home under a pile of dirty clothes as his phone beeped repeatedly. There was a sandalwood scented incense burning on the dresser, trying to cover up the smell of weed. His room had several piles of clothes, each dirtier than the previous, with sheets that were no longer white and bordered on mustard yellow. The light from the window peeked in through the broken mini blinds, also covered in dust. It was Ruben blowing his phone up. He knew what he wanted, and David was not sure if he wanted to give it to him. Ever since his last visit to Pops' house, he was avoiding Ruben, figuring he was angry with him. David was madder at himself than anyone else.

Pops texted David about some work he had for him while he had been at Ruben's the weekend before he found out about Pops' death. Ruben kept pestering him about who was texting him.

Ruben's living room had a sunken floor and a long glass centre table in the middle spanning half the distance of the area. Under it was a purple and yellow rug, dotted with burn marks. The table itself had several hotel trays where Ruben kept all his paraphernalia in place. End tables and desks filled the outer part of the living area, where his sound system and record player were located. A light level of Fleetwood Mac's "Warm Ways" was on repeat. Ruben and David both sat on the only couch stuck together at the hip.

"Fucker, put the phone down and grab this oiler. It will not smoke itself."

"Give me a sec," said David.

"Who's fucking texting you? Some trick."

"Stop it. It's Pops. He has some work for me."

"Some work, huh?"

"Yeah, he needs me to mow his lawn."

"Why are you doing that shit, anyway?"

"I don't mind working for my money."

Ruben slapped David's ass.

"I know you don't, baby."

"Stop it, please. I mean it. Anyway, I just answered him back. I'm gonna go over there in the morning, so we can't party too late, okay?"

David could see in Ruben's face that his mood changed and didn't know why it bothered him so much he was doing yard work.

"Yeah, sure."

Ruben excused himself to the restroom and left David alone in the living room.

David grabbed the pipe on the table and loaded it with the crystal that was already in the glass candy dish; lit it and took one long dragon breath before sinking back into the couch. His skin tingled, and his face experienced flushing because of the rush of chemicals hitting him. Before the rush was over, he took another long hit from the pipe. Before he exhaled, Ruben came back into the room with a new pipe in hand.

"Take this. It's a new batch I got in yesterday. You gotta try it."

"Uh, alright, but what's the difference?"

Ruben cleaned the outside bowl of the pipe and lit it with the light from his cell phone.

"You see, the crystals are denser and pack a harder punch. I took a hit. It's fucking good. Hit it."

Ruben handed the pipe to David, who looked skeptical.

"And you're sure it's safe?"

"Yes, babe, I just tried it a second ago."

Ruben flicked the torch on and hovered it under the bowl.

"Smoke, don't let it go to waste. I'll tell you when to stop."

David took a large breath into his nose and exhaled before placing his lips on the pipe. When he did, he slowly inhaled the smoke. The circular motion of the smoke as it left the bowl and into the stem reminded him of how thunderclouds look when they are forming. The lighter and darker colours of the cloud mixing and forming another shade.

Instantly, when the smoke hit his mouth, he knew something was different. It tasted sweeter than normal. Ruben kept the torch under the bowl so much that all the crystal melted and formed a pool that filled the bowl almost midway. He never seen so much crystal melted down before. It was intoxicating, and he wanted to smoke until he couldn't.

David's slow inhale enabled him to take in more than he normally could, and after seven seconds, his lungs became filled even though he tried to keep it in as much as he could, but his lungs burst out the smoke only after three seconds. Ruben's smile got even bigger, displacing the pipe in another drawer. Usually, Ruben would have hit the pipe after him, but this time, he didn't.

David felt lightheaded and dizzy. The room spun around him. His skin no longer felt flush, and his body felt numb. There was a tingling sensation that began in his toes, but as it shot up his body, it suddenly stopped at his mid-torso. David tried to speak, but was having a hard time controlling his mouth. From the corner of his eye, he saw Ruben texting someone on his phone and smoking a different pipe.

Wondering if Ruben did something to his pipe because the couch seemed to melt under him and when he glanced up, he noticed the ceiling fan came on which he didn't notice before. His skin seemed to warm up and David felt lightheaded, more than usual. It was different this time; the smoke smelled like burning plastic bags. His eyelids became heavier, and David had a hard time focusing on his breathing.

"Babe?"

"Shhh, baby. It's okay. You just got a powerful hit. You'll be okay. Just keep lying down and enjoy the ride."

"But I can't feel my legs. I don't feel normal."

Before Ruben responded, David saw glows of colours around Ruben and himself. They pulsated in different shapes and shades. His hands clammed up, and his breathing seemed too shallow. David was obviously having trouble breathing, but Ruben didn't seem to be concerned with it. Instead, he was on the phone. David kicked the table over with his leg to get his attention.

"Damn, you dropped all the shit. It's okay. I'm gonna take you to a friend's place. The guy's a nurse and can take care of you while I take care of some business."

<hr>

DAVID DIDN'T WANT TO GO ANYWHERE FEELING HOW he felt, but he had little choice in the matter and was in no shape to fight what was happening to him. Ruben carried him to his car, and they drove off. David's head laid back on the passenger seat slanted back. In this position, he could only see the tree line and power lines as they drove off to an unknown destination.

Finally, the lights diminished, and crickets and frogs

replaced the sounds of the city. The sloshing water against the banks was audible. When the car stopped, Ruben came around and opened the door and unbuckled him, then carried him to a nearby cabin.

Julio, Ruben's friend, opened the door and motioned him into a bedroom. Once tucked under the sheets in a bed, David slowly felt the sensation in his legs return. The colours around the room didn't go away yet. Even though he couldn't see well yet, he got a glimpse at Julio, who reminded him of his Pilipino co-worker from Benny's, except this guy was much stockier and way paler. His hair had dark brown tight curls, and his eyebrows were bushy to match. Either the guy had gotten off shift or he wore scrubs at home, but he had a pair of lime green scrubs from head to toe that David noticed before his vision gave out.

"Thanks, Julio. Just watch him overnight. I have something I need to do and don't want him alone."

"What happened to him? What did he take?" asked Julio.

Ruben reached into his pocket and pulled out a small baggie and used his fingers to spell out the letters PCP. Julio audibly gasped, and before he could say anything, Ruben covered his mouth.

"Say nothing to him about it. The boy had it coming. Just watch him till I get back."

"I don't know if I feel comfortable watching him in his condition. That stuff is so unpredictable. We really should take him to a hospital ER, not here."

"I want him here. Besides, you owe me one. Have you forgotten?"

Julio glanced down.

"Of course I haven't."

"Good then. Watch him. Give him fluids or whatever. You're the nurse, not me. Just take care of him and don't let him leave. I'll be back."

"Fine, go."

David was staring out the window when he saw Ruben peek into the room he was in. His body wanted to look toward him and give him a piece of his mind, shouting at the top of his lungs how violated he felt, but he couldn't move. Ruben gave him a peck on the cheek.

"That tickles."

Even though David spoke, he still could not direct his eyes toward Ruben. From the corner of his eye, he saw Ruben leave the cabin. Outside the window, he glimpsed at Ruben enter his car. He seemed to wait for something, but after a couple of minutes passed, he received a phone call. David watched his demeanour change, and a smile appeared. For what? David had no clue. It couldn't be anything good.

13

Inside his home office, Ruben grabbed his burner phone from the drawer of his desk. His office was tucked away off to the back of his home with a view of the living room from the doorway. A sole lamp took the corner space next to the oak desk. With the burner phone, he dialled.

"Salinas. I got something I need you to do," Ruben said as he thumbed through the books on his shelf.

"What? It's kind of a bad time."

"Stop complaining. I need a background check run."

"Why? For what," said Salinas.

"It doesn't matter. All you need to know is that I need it done, okay?"

"It's getting harder for me to do things with no one asking questions. I don't want to get burned," said Salinas.

"You worry too much. It's just a simple background check. Are you ready for the name?"

"What is it?" said Salinas.

"Santos Morelo. The guy lives on 1217 Basin Circle in Valley City."

"Wait. You mean Coach Morelo? The same guy?"

"Yes, and?"

"Why do you need a background check run on him?"

"Salinas, it's better if you ask no more questions. You don't hear me asking you questions about your business. Just get it done and email me it when it comes in."

"It might take a day or so, but I'll email it when it comes through."

Salinas paused.

"I got to say, Ruben. I'm not sure how much longer we can have this arrangement. It seems like I'm pushing the limits. I'm making too many official requests without official reasons for them. It's inevitable I will be caught."

"Just get this done for me, and I'll settle your debt, but you better come through, okay?"

"Don't worry, you'll get it."

IN THE MORNING, RUBEN WOKE TO HIS PHONE'S email notification. Being more comfortable, he moved from his office to his den. Ruben still had a tiny workspace with a fire walled computer but also a pullout couch and 60-inch tv on the wall for when the mood struck. The room had carpeted floors containing several Kashan Rugs, which he purchased over the years that he really liked, and he especially loved the centre piece Emerald Green runner rug spanning the length of the room. It was a modern floral design with interconnecting rose petals and bordered design that cost him over five thousand dollars. The room was his perfect little hideaway from everything and everyone.

Finally, Salinas came through. Before he left his bed, he grabbed the pipe and torch from his nightstand and took two quick puffs and inhaled the vapour, holding it in. Afterward, his eyes widened, and the grogginess of the morning dissipated.

At this desk, he turned on his PC. Ruben scrolled through the laundry list of programs until he found Ghost VPN. After he engaged it and brought up a private window, he found Salinas' email. It contained all the basic items you would expect to be in a background check: driving and criminal record, along with something else that Ruben wasn't expecting, his medical history. It showed Santos suffered from a minor heart attack a few months prior and was on Toprol, a beta blocker that helps with blood circulation to help with the symptoms. This gave Ruben an idea. He headed over to Santos' home to track his movements.

When he arrived at his neighbourhood, he found it mostly quiet and empty of traffic. Most of the surrounding houses seemed vacant except for his direct neighbour to his left. He parked several houses down in front of one of the abandoned homes. Keeping track of Santos' departures and arrivals, he noted the duration of his absences. When the lights went out and when they turned on in the morning, he made a note to be sure to get his schedule down exactly.

After two days of observations and an eight ball of T, Ruben felt he had gotten his schedule down. Planning to enter the house in the evening when Santos left for two solid hours was his goal. When the time came, Santos left like clockwork, and the house became silent. He parked his car around the back near his vacant neighbour's covered parking spot. As soon as the sun had set, he made his way to the backyard and to his back door. Despite the back door being locked, it was missing a deadbolt. A simple plastic card jiggled it open. The home was dark and void of sound.

Inside the kitchen, he placed his gloves on and looked through the cabinets, but found no medications. In the back bedrooms, he had no luck either. In the bathroom, there was an array of pill bottles on the sink and in the medicine cabinet. Most were vitamins and fish oil pills, but he found two bottles of prescription medications. One was baby aspirin, and the other was what he had been looking for: Toprol; opening it and grabbing several in his hand, he placed them in a small plastic container he had brought with him. After he replaced the bottles back in their spots, he left the home and ensured everything looked as it had before he came in.

Once he made it back home, he grabbed his burner again from his office desk, dialled Roger, a connection of his. Ruben squeezed a view from the blinds and could not see movement outside. Someone's car alarm was going off in the distance. Shutting off the lamp, he retreated to his desk and sat in darkness while waiting for Roger to answer.

"Rog. Do you still got that pill press we used last year for those janky Xanax pills we made?" asked Ruben.

"I still got it. Why, what's up?"

"I need a favour. I got some pills that I need you to duplicate, but I need something else going inside of them. Can you help me out?"

"Alright, alright. I see what you trying to do. And what do you want inside of them instead?"

"Just powdered crystal."

"I can see where you're going with this. Alright, I think I can swing that for you."

"If you can take care of this for me, there's an eight-ball of T in it for you. You down?"

Ruben sat up from the chair he was sitting on and waited for Roger to answer. He could hear a passing train in the background and loud thumping music playing.

"Hell, yeah. I got you."

"I'll have someone drop off the pills and your ball later today. I'm gonna have Salinas drop by and pick them up when they're ready, alright?"

"No sweat. I'll hit you up when they're done."

"Thanks, man."

After hanging up, he called Julio, who told him that David was still resting and was looking better. Ruben told him he would be by in the morning to grab David. He reloaded his pipe with a single shard of crystal that had to be loaded through the stem because of its size. After melting it, it nearly overflowed into the stem, but Ruben's inhaling kept it in place. His eyes glazed, and his cheeks blossomed a pink hue. It was as if his bones liquified like the crystal, making him float for the rest of the night.

14

BACK AT THE STATION, CARLOS BEGAN HIS RESEARCH on Ruben. If he followed his trail, something had to come up. Santos must have had his card in his home for a reason. Things just don't happen at random. Carlos didn't believe in chance. He searched on the internet for any information he could find on Ruben. All that came up was his professional business profile on the Valley City Chamber of Commerce. Ruben sat on the board of several local charities, including the Boys and Girls Club. His Facebook page had nothing suspicious and appeared like any typical business advertising on the site. Carlos was getting upset he was coming up empty-handed.

Carlos took a break and head to the break room to grab some coffee and a sour cream donut from the pantry. He got Captain Rankin to listen to him about one thing, making sure fresh pastries from Shipley's Donuts were available every day. Of course, when the captain first started bringing them in, he took all the credit. Carlos didn't really mind as long as his favourite sour cream donuts kept coming.

Inside the break room, he found a corner seat near the refrigerator and stared at the *"Wall of Giving"* that Shelly created from payroll last spring. It displayed pictures of anyone in the station who had done any type of philanthropy work. Month after month, the same handful of people kept showing up in the pictures. Ronny from the back office, Jorge from sanitation, and so forth. Although he noticed Salinas was in several of these pictures. He never thought of him as much as a charitable man. He always kept to himself, and they hardly ever spoke. Most times, it was out of necessity.

Carlos finished his donut and coffee and moved closer to the wall to get a better look. Several photos captured Salinas at the local Boys and Girls Club, where he made a donation to their sports department. They listed Salinas as a co-sponsor of the donating team. It was the same for all the pictures he was in. It couldn't have been a coincidence both Salinas and Ruben were involved in the same charity. He looked into it further and headed back to his desk. Before calling the Boys and Girls Club, he ran a background check on Ruben to find more information that he could dig up. While it processed, he dialled up the club and spoke to their head of donations, Missy.

"Good afternoon, my name is Detective Alvarado, and I am doing some research on some of your donors. Are you familiar with the donations made on behalf of the Valley City PD?"

"I can definitely try to assist you, Detective. I am familiar with the program. What information is it you need?"

"I am trying to get a complete list of donors attached to the program. I understand there are privacy considerations, but my case depends on verifying this information. Is there any way you can help me?"

"I would really like to help you, Detective, but our donor list is completely private. Only our donors can provide permission to release their names to the public. Unless we have that form on file, I won't be able to help."

"Can you check anyway, please?"

"Sure, give me a second."

The silence while on hold made Carlos feel even further away from finding anything of concrete value. Usually, there was Muzak, something to distract his brain from thinking of the worse. Instead, he was alone in his thoughts and only thought of how things would turn out for the worse, how it would take time to ask for a warrant, time he didn't have. Sealing those files for privacy and without evidence would make it look bad, and his case would be dead on arrival.

He didn't want to fail Henry.

"Thank you for waiting. I'm back, Detective. Okay, here is what I found. Most of our donor list has kept their names private, except for two. I'll have to check with our back-office team and see if the redacted information is available on the read-only file on our server. Can I get the information to you later today or tomorrow at the latest?"

Carlos stood motionless and could not speak for a moment. Did he get some useful information? It wasn't much, but it was a place to start.

"Yes, thank you. I appreciate your help. You can reach me at the number I called you at or just call the station and ask for me. Goodbye."

For now, he needed to see if those redacted names were in fact Salinas and Ruben. It wasn't a stretch to think they would be involved in the same charity organization, which wasn't anything incriminating. It would show that they had an association with each other. Although it could be something harmless, it still required further investigation. He would have to wait until Missy and the background check came back in tomorrow for more clarification. Carlos investigated something that Ruben had told him about his former relationship with Mr. Morelo. He pulled up the department's webpage on their softball team Santos was a part of, as well as Ruben.

He scrolled through the pictures from the past several years, and in all the pictures with the team, he found Santos labeled as *'coach.'* Down toward the bottom of the picture gallery, he found a section called administrative volunteers. In it, he found dozens of pictures of Ruben donating the team's uniforms, with several members of the department as its representative. In the last three years, he found the representative on the police side was Salinas. There he was again, Salinas and Ruben in the same organization. Carlos couldn't believe that it was all a coincidence again. There must be something there.

He had to keep digging.

He searched around the detective's section and found Salinas still at his desk. Contemplating, approaching him and asking him point blank about his connection to Ruben and if he knew what happened to Santos. If he asked him directly and didn't have solid evidence, he would get stonewalled and give away the element of surprise he currently had. Instead, Carlos approached him and asked for help on his case and see how he responded to his questions and theories. He locked his computer and walked over to Salinas' desk.

"Salinas, you got a minute?"

Startled, Salinas glanced up and seemed surprised when he saw Carlos.

"Alvarado. Sure, how can I help?"

"I've hit a wall in this case I'm working on. I would appreciate a fresh pair of eyes on it. Do you mind?"

He motioned for Carlos to take a seat at his desk.

"Yeah, go for it."

"Alright, so I'm working on Coach Morelo's cause of death. You remember him?"

"Yeah, he coached our team every summer. It's a shame what happened."

"My only lead right now is a business card that was left at the scene from a local business owner, Ruben Delgado. Ring a bell?"

"Um, no. Should it?"

Carlos waited a second before answering him. He wanted to see the reaction on Salinas' face and how his body language reacted. He seemed calm mostly, except every time their eyes met, Salinas glimpsed in another direction.

"No, not at all. Just thought I would throw it out there. So, I did some research on this Ruben and found him to be involved in a lot of local charities, including our softball team and others. Nothing shady so far, but I'm just getting started. Any ideas on where else to look?"

"I mean, did you check his police record? That's usually a good place to start. If it comes back clean, then at least you know he's likely on the straight and narrow, you know?"

"I did request that. I'm running it now. We don't have any local arrests, but I'm checking state and federal as well. I'm also creating a short list of known associates to interview. Like I said, I'm just getting started."

"Sounds like you are on track. Don't know much else I can offer you."

"Well, anything you can think of, send it my way, and thanks for the extra set of eyes."

He tapped Salinas on the back and headed back to his desk. Sitting down, he wondered why Salinas didn't disclose his prior relationship with Ruben. He probably figured Carlos hadn't dug that deep yet. No matter the reason, he knew now Salinas had something to hide, and so did Ruben.

Carlos glanced back at Salinas' desk and noticed he was staring at his monitor without typing. He almost had a blank stare with no emotion to it. Then suddenly, as if instructed, he began typing like a madman on his computer.

Click, Click, Click, Space, Click, Space

From his vantage point, Carlos couldn't see what he was typing, but his face gave away a sense of urgency. Salinas' brow crunched, and his eyes scanned the computer screen, line by line. His watch beeped, and he stopped typing. Something must have popped up on his smart watch for him to have stopped typing. He then turned off his monitor and talked to the captain.

Carlos couldn't make out what they were saying, but whatever was said was quick. Within two minutes, Salinas was out of his office and out the door. Carlos wondered where he was off to and when he would return. He glanced around the room and the clock on the wall: 5:16 p.m. Most of the detectives had left for the day, and by the looks of it, the captain was on the way out too. Soon he would be alone in the detective's section.

Once everyone left, Carlos made his way to Salina's desk. Before touching anything, he put his nitrile gloves on. Salinas' computer was still on. Carlos clicked on the monitor, and a screensaver of a cat and dog hugging came on. With a tap of the mouse, it disappeared, and his desktop showed up. Carlos wondered how someone of Salinas' tenure failed to have a password on his computer. It would seem Salinas was a trusting person.

He moused around his screen, looking for his email program, but found none. Opening up the internet, he found the last page loading. Mail.com came up with an account already logged in. He scrolled through the inbox and found nothing strange. In fact, there was only a handful of emails back and forth between Salinas and an email user named 'hielo2001.'

Carlos pulled his notepad out of his pocket and wrote the

email address and domain. He made one more glance around the room and found it still empty and trafficless. The contents of the emails seemed to be coded, but from what Carlos gathered, Salinas was passing information to the email name about something or someone coded *'Eld.'* Again, he jotted the name down and returned his notebook to his pocket. He searched the rest of his computer and desk but found nothing.

After closing the browser and returning Salinas' desk to the way he found it, he turned off the monitor and returned even more determined to find a connection between Ruben, Salinas, and Santos.

15

It was unusual for Ruben to spend much time outdoors, but Valley City offered a sunny, warm day, and he would not let it go to waste. Outside in his backyard near his pool, he laid down to soak in the sun. The fences around his backyard stood at an impressive seven feet. To discourage outsiders from peering in, he had a line of Sabal palms lining the fence all the way around, circling the pool. His phone rang: Salinas calling him back. Ruben's forehead wrinkled and became annoyed at being bothered.

"What do you need?"

From the phone line, he heard car horns and people arguing about their orders being wrong. Ruben got accustomed to Salinas using his usual spot at McDonald's on Grimes Boulevard across from the UPS store. Him being there; he knew something must have happened.

"Your special project is done, and I have dropped them off at your lockbox."

"Good. Anything else?"

"That's all."

Without saying a word, Ruben hung up the phone and

shut it off. Before he needed to go anywhere, he still had thirty more minutes of sunbathing, so he closed his eyes and drifted away.

A COUPLE OF HOURS LATER, AFTER THE SUN WENT down, Ruben headed over to the UPS store next to the old Blockbuster from eons ago. After leaving the gated access of Treasure Hills, Ruben headed down South Commerce Street running the length of Valley City, almost bisecting it like a 90-degree angle.

Commerce street was one of the oldest streets in Valley City, dating back to its founding, which gave the drive a more scenic view. As Ruben entered the downtown district, an array of old mom and pop shops littered the area from Lacks' furniture to Betty's Thrift Shop and an old staple of Valley City, El Taquito Café.

Once he passed the downtown district, he arrived at a more industrial part of Valley City, where time had not been so kind. There were various abandoned warehouses and in the middle of this ghostly area of town was the UPS store. Given the location, as Ruben parked, he scanned the parking lot and found the area to be deserted minus a cat or two running in the distance.

Unsure if the storm was approaching or receding, he was taken by surprise at the soft, rolling thunder in the distance. With the air seeming brisker, it gave more credence to the former instead of the latter. The store offered a service with a twenty-four-hour access lockbox. All that was needed was his key, and he could come and go as he pleased at any hour. There was no one around. He spent only a fraction of a minute inside collecting his special project.

Once in hand, he compared the time to his notes on

Santos' schedule and found that he would be out that night for two hours, as he did every Thursday. It really didn't matter where he went; what was important was his window of opportunity.

Leaving the warehouse district, he returned down commerce street and headed south this time. As the warehouse district thinned out and the area became more populous and traffic thickened, the surrounding neighbourhoods seemed to go from bad to worse.

The houses around him were in disrepair and falling apart and then the next neighbourhood changed to government housing that reminded Ruben of matchstick homes all uniform and without style. Children could be seen playing among the drying clothes on the old-style clotheslines. Ruben smirked at the kids and honked his horn several times, giving them a scare not being fond of kids either.

Arriving at Wichita Street, he made the turn past the train tracks down to Santos' neighbourhood. When he arrived at Basin Circle, Santos' truck was already gone, and the lights dimmed inside. He sat in his car two houses down, as he did before, and observed his neighbours. There didn't seem to be any activity on the street, so he made his way to the backyard.

As before, there was no sign of life from his only neighbour. Using a plastic card, Ruben opened the backdoor and moved in. The house seemed as if nothing changed since he last visited. It was dark and calm, and the air became so still he almost choked on it. In the bathroom cabinet, he found the pills where he left them.

Before replacing them, he counted them to replace the same amount. The real pills went into his pocket and added the fake ones into Santos' container, then placed it back in the cabinet. After leaving the house, he sat in his car for a moment before remembering he needed to pick up David at Julio's and did not want to be late.

On the way to Julio's, Ruben noticed the lake level rose after last week's rains. Tree shadows raced across the hood of his white Mercedes as he drove through a heavily wooded lake area, where an abundance of boats skimmed the surface.

As he got closer to Julio's, which was at the far most point of the lake, the boat traffic lessened, allowing for remoteness and privacy. His closest neighbour was two miles away. No one lived opposite him. When he arrived, David was already outside on the porch, smoking a cigarette, and Julio was nowhere around.

"Babe, you're up. Feeling better," asked Ruben.

"What the fuck happened? What was in that shit I smoked?"

"David, calm down. I'll explain everything, but where's Julio?"

"I don't know. Inside or something. Why?"

"Just asking. This is his place, and you are out here all alone."

"I don't care about Julio. Ruben, I'm not in the mood and don't appreciate you talking down to me. I've had it with you. This entire thing has gotten out of control. YOU have gotten out of control. I still can't believe what you did and then dumping me here with a stranger. This has got to stop."

Ruben studied David as his emotions were getting the better of him. His eyes were welling up and his hands were forming fists.

"David, I don't know what you are trying to accomplish with all that bluster, but you better calm your ass down. I don't need you embarrassing me in front of Julio. Got it?"

Ruben saw that David did not like that statement one bit as he was now pacing back and forth and flicked his cigarette at his feet.

"Me, embarrass you? You've got to be kidding me. That's it, I've had it. Are you ready to go? I don't want to be here anymore. It's creepy out here and the sound of crickets and frogs makes me paranoid. I hate it. Let's go, NOW!!"

"Watch your tone, babe, if you know what's good for you."

"Enough Ruben, just open the fucking car! I'm done! Do whatever you fucking want without me. I'm through!"

Now Ruben was getting agitated and didn't feel like dealing with David at the moment, so he opened the car with his keys.

"There you happy? Let me tell Julio we are heading out. Meet me at the car."

Ruben knocked on Julio's door. A few seconds later, Julio appeared.

"Hey. Thanks for the assist. I'm sorry if you heard any of that. David's being a little bitch about all this. We are going to be heading out. By the way, your debt has been cleared. Thanks."

"Sure, and thank you. Hey, are you sure he's going to be, ok? I mean, he doesn't seem to be in the best of moods."

"Julio, I said your debt is paid. Don't make me rethink that. And mind your own damn business," Ruben snapped.

Without saying goodbye, Julio closed the door on Ruben. Inside the car, David seemed eager to find out what happened to him the other night. As they drove back to town, this time, David saw his surroundings, unlike his arrival trip. Ruben watched him as he looked out at the lake, admiring the number of boats that zoomed back and forth. The quietness of the car ride made Ruben feel uneasy.

"Are you going to make me ask you again—what happened?"

Ruben flipped the visor up and lowered the satellite radio, letting out a sigh of relief.

"This is really all your fault, babe, you know?"

"My fault? How do you figure?"

"Ever since you started hanging out with that Santos guy, you have been coming over less and less. It pissed me off."

"What are you talking about?"

"I told you before, you are *my* piece of ass. No one else's."

"Are you serious? Are you fucking high? Wait, of course you're high. But what does this have to do with what happened to me the other night?"

Ruben slowed his speech down and articulated his words.

"I couldn't let you keep spending time over there without some sort of consequence."

"Spit it out, Ruben. I don't like these games."

"That shit you smoked. I laced your crystal with PCP."

"You're fucking crazy. I could have died, you idiot."

"You were never in danger. That's why I got Julio on call, for shit like this. I took care of you."

"It doesn't feel like that to me."

Silence filled the car again, and neither one of them wanted to speak first. The windows in the car became covered in condensation as the temperature lowered. Ruben saw David's knees shivering, and it made him happy inside, but he kept his smile to himself and remained solemn instead. His car was immaculately clean, not even a trace of a gum wrapper. Through the rearview mirror, Ruben eyed his backseat that was lined with a St. Jude blanket.

"Okay, look. Shit like this only happens if you disrespect me and our relationship. You hear me? I don't want to cut you off again like last time. You were sick for weeks after that."

"Don't you dare do that to me again. I can't handle it."

"Then you got to stop spending time there. I don't want you seeing anyone else."

"It's not like that. I'm just mowing his lawn for cash."

"It's okay. You don't need to do that. I got you covered, you know that."

Ruben could tell David felt defeated. He was staring at his

feet and watched him scrape his feet along the carpet protector. It resembled chalk powder on cement, and he continued playing with it.

"I know that, babe, but sometimes it just feels good to have some cash of my own. You know?"

"I do. How about you clean the pool, and I'll pay for that? Fair?"

"I guess so. I'm just scared you're going to lace my stuff again."

"You don't have to worry about that, as long as you do what I ask. It's win-win."

"Alright, well, we are getting close to my house. Before you get on my street, can you drop me off at the corner? I don't want my brother seeing us."

"Sure, sure. I got you."

Down one street, he walked past Mrs. Zuniga's house. Outside her patio sat two tabby cats play fighting with each other. Her house was the rare one painted in yellow and green, unlike the neighbours, which mostly coloured their homes in blues and whites. She even refused to take down her Hillary 2020 sign. The cats continued to fight until one of them got tired and gave up, giving in to the other. Ruben creepily watched David enter his home and the lights turn off a minute later.

Inside, David found the house quiet, except for Mr. Hamster rolling away in his cage's wheel. Judging from the utter silence, David assumed his brother must be asleep because of the late hour. All he wanted to do was throw himself down on his bed, but he was starving.

David scrounged around the fridge and couldn't find anything fast to make except a couple of frozen turnovers.

After nuking them in the microwave and grabbing some juice, he retreated to his room. The turnovers were devoured in no time. To avoid waking his brother, he closed his door gently and undressed himself so he could shower, hoping he wanted to take the literal stink off himself.

As he stared at himself in the mirror before showering, his collar bones protruded from under his skin in a sickly shape. He was never one to work out or be in good shape, but looking like a skeleton couldn't be a good thing. His eyes seemed to be more sunken in than normal and the colour of his skin seemed off.

Suddenly, a fitful rage from deep inside of him emerged, and it almost caused him to break the mirror in front of him, but he took out his frustration on himself. David repeatedly pounded on his chest and the back of head many times over until the pain of the day wore off.

The truth David was realizing is the pain would not likely wear off soon and the one to blame was Ruben, but he was partially to blame as well. The addiction was out of control, but until now it did not affect his outside life or others. Almost dying, hadn't even registered with David or even the thought of seeking help from his brother. David wanted to avoid judgement at all costs because he knew Carlos would lead with judgement and that's the last thing he needed now.

After his thoughts quieted for a bit, he showered and dressed himself in boxers and shorts for bed. He hadn't had time to clean his room since getting fired at Benny's, so his room was still a disaster zone. With his bed covered in clothes, he made room to sleep by shoving them off to the corner between the wall and his bed. Out of sight, out of mind, he thought. As he lay there fiddling with his short drawstrings, his thoughts returned to Ruben.

How did he let things get so far down the rabbit hole with him and had he passed the point of no return? By asking that question, did he still have a chance to come out the other side of it clean?

Drugs made him feel like a yo-yo. When he wasn't smoking, he wanted to, and when he was smoking, he wanted more. Sometimes, even when David had his fill, and would swear off it for a few days, the slightest reminder of it would tumble him back into its ugly grip and the cycle would start all over again. It's a pattern he knew too well, and David knew too that Ruben used it to his advantage to keep him at his side.

Thinking about it made him feel ugly and just plain used. The sad part about it is that even though David felt like this now, given the right circumstance and the availability of meth, it would all change, making him go headfirst back with Ruben in a heartbeat if it meant he could smoke. David felt hopeless and knew Ruben had him where he wanted him.

His head was hurting at the thought of it, so instead of thinking, he shut his brain off by hitting his bong and smoking some Northern Lights he picked up the other day hoping it would put him to sleep, leaving today's problems for tomorrow.

***

It was two days, and Ruben was back home, logged into his computer. He opened his VPN and Tor once again before heading to his email account, signing up for a temporary account that would only exist for the duration of the message, and which would be virtually untraceable. In the body, he selected the time delay feature and set for delivery in twenty-four hours.

Minimizing the window, he brought up the Valley City PD website and found the contact list for their detectives. Scrolling down the pages until he found David's brother, and, under his profile, he found his email address, and finally copied it to his clipboard.

Ruben paused before pasting the email address and looked at one of the rare pictures of David he had on his phone. It was from early in their relationship. David was standing on the shores of Valley City Lake, holding a fishing pole. Ruben had forgotten in the beginning they went out on an actual date before the meth took hold. His wave of nostalgia only lasted a few moments before he germanely deleted the photo from his phone.

Across the room, on the wall, he saw his reflection in the mirror and found his emotional armour seemed to crack and that was something which couldn't be happening. Ruben opened on the desk drawer and grabbed his oiler and torch and inhaled a long deep hit of the chemical burn that soon washed away any sense of emotional turmoil he might have been having and instead turned his attention back to the task at hand, teaching David a lesson.

Carlos' email address was pasted, and he began writing the body of the email.

Dear Mr. Alvarado,

It pains me to inform you of your brother's actions, but it must be done. Before you wonder who I am, I am without a name, but sufficed to say I am a concerned party.

I regret to inform you I have been witness to your brother's demise in the excess of crystal meth. Several days ago, your brother nearly died and overdosed on the drug. I was able to get him help and a safe place to recover, but I feel it has gone too far and David is in danger of overdosing again.

With a clear conscience, I cannot be around him while he behaves in this manner as I do not want to be party to his death. I am reaching out to you since you are his family and a member of law enforcement. Perhaps you can reach him before it is too late. What broke the camel's back was his involvement in the death of Santos Morelo.

During one of his low points, David confessed to me he broke into Santos's home to steal money that Santos kept hidden in the home that he had encountered on a previous visit. When he couldn't find the money, he took revenge on Santos and swapped his heart pills for ones filled with crystal meth. Where he got the fake pills, I have no clue, just he said he got them from some friend of his.

I am sorry to bring this to you, but I felt you deserved to know the truth about your brother. Hopefully, you can help him before it's too late.

Sincerely,

A Concerned party

Even though it was for selfish reasons, Ruben wanted Carlos to know the truth. How he handled that information was up to him, as long as it created chaos. Plus, he needed to teach David a lesson about how he acted the other day in the car. David complied with what Ruben wanted, but there should have been no rebuttal period in Ruben's eyes. Complete and utter control over David was what he wanted, and this email would be his nail in the coffin.

Once he finished, he made sure not to leave any evidence of his identity, and since the email address was masked, Carlos would have no way of knowing who sent the email.

Ruben pushed send.

Tomorrow, David's life would change for the worse. With a smile on his face, Ruben brought out the bong and inhaled a massive hit before slowly releasing the vapour into the room, basking in its warmth.

16

Needing a break from being indoors and because he was getting hungry, Carlos headed out for a bite to eat to see if inspiration struck him elsewhere. He wasn't sure what he was in the mood for, so he let the drive down Commerce street give him some ideas. Carlos passed Benny's, WhataBite and various other chain restaurants, but he wasn't in the mood for those.

The evolving relationship between Ruben and Salinas intertwined with his thoughts on food. His research came to a standstill, but his gut told him there was something more. He also told him it needed to be refilled.

Up ahead, he saw his salvation, Starlite Burger. The bright neon red and blue lights spreading across the building like a beacon on the street were always a favourite of Carlos' growing up. It was one of the few things that his family could agree on to eat on the weekends before Amanda's death. Everyone would get their own 2-piece chicken combo with fries. Carlos could still taste the grease from the bags that always leaked and caused stains on his clothes.

Before his mouth salivated, he pulled into the Starlite

Burger and went up the outside window to order. As he exited the vehicle, he heard his computer's email icon beep, showing a message, but waited to read after he got his food. His hunger would wait for no one.

Carlos scanned the menu, but he already knew what he wanted. His memory of chicken and fries was so fresh anything else would be sacrilegious. The lady at the counter whose voice could rival Marge from the Simpsons in scratchiness hurried him along with my order, treating him like there were twenty people behind him when, in fact, there was none.

Carlos let it go and gave her a big tip because who knows if her day was going bad. A little niceness can go a long way. Standing near the hood of his vehicle, Carlos smelt the potato grease flow in the air and buttered buns as well.

Inside the restaurant, near the fountain drinks children were playing with the soda dispensers and letting ice easily fall out without the workers noticing. Parents were oblivious as well. It made Carlos chuckle.

Three shrill *ding ding ding* interrupted Carlos' train of thought as his food was now ready. Even from his distance, the grease was glistening in all its glory. He grabbed his box and an exorbitant number of napkins before heading back to his vehicle.

Smiling at his food, he inhaled his chicken pieces and left no meat on the bone. Doing so left little room for fries, but he pushed through for the sake of taste. When he was done, his computer's email notification dinged again and this time he intended to open it, but not before cleaning his hands free from grease.

Once he used his hand sanitizer, he clicked opened his email. There were several spam messages he deleted, but one sender he didn't recognize but the subject piqued his interest because it had his name and his brother's as well.

As he read it, the colour in his face dropped, the taut in his body loosened, and the food in his stomach was now beginning to spin cycles, as if it was a washing machine. David was using drugs. He was involved in Santos' death. How could all of this be possible? Could be the connection Carlos was searching for all this time be his own brother David?

It just didn't make sense to Carlos. This accusation of swapping out pills was a serious one and was something he needed to understand, but could it be true? How could all this be going on all under his own roof and Carlos never even suspected it and who was this concerned party?

This raised more questions than it answered. Carlos would now have to verify these claims, check the pills, look for prints, look for eyewitness reports, and check the toxicology reports. It didn't look good for David.

He loved his brother, but he knew justice needed to come first, even if it meant putting his brother last.

17

Back home, David finally answered Ruben's incessant calls and texts from the previous night. There were sixteen missed calls and thirty-two text messages which came in. It became excessive and was the only reason he bothered to reply at all. Instead of texting him, he dialled his number.

"Thank god you called. I was worried about you."

"You were worried about me?"

David hated it when Ruben played the concerned boyfriend. It suited him only when he wanted something from David.

"Of course I was. Are you feeling better? Got some sleep?"

"I got some sleep but stop detracting from what happened."

Ruben breathed hard as he stayed silent and waited for him to say more. His old tricks would not fly with David any longer.

"I'm still royally pissed at what you did. It was possible for me to have died. Playing games with my life is something I dislike about you. I'm not a fucking toy, Ruben."

David usually called him babe, wanting to make a point,

he crossed a line, causing Ruben to remain silent. The only noise heard was a slight cough, as if he was clearing his throat, readying to speak.

"If you say nothing, then I think I'm through with you. It's not funny anymore, and I am tired of your shit."

Ruben made a clicking noise with his tongue before speaking.

"I was waiting for you to stop whining about what happened. I thought I clarified the reason it happened was because of who you were hanging out with, and as long as it stopped, you would have nothing to worry about anymore."

"That's not the point. You use me like I am some sort of piece of meat...worse, property...that you can treat however you want."

"Exactly. You're my piece of meat. I'm going to make it easy, and I never want to discuss this again. You stop hanging out with anyone else, or I will cut you off completely and make it impossible for anyone in town to sell to you. You will have to go cold turkey."

"You don't have to threaten me. This is exactly what I mean. I don't like this attitude of yours."

David thought back to how he first met Ruben. The man caused his world to turn upside down. The crystal held power over him unlike anything he ever experienced before. David tried other drugs before, and none of them were like crystal. From the first time he took that puff, it had control over him he couldn't understand.

When he wasn't high, he was thinking of getting high, and when he was high, he was thinking about his next hit. It became impossible to manage. No amount of weed would ever make that feeling go away. When Ruben threatened to cut him off, part of him wanted to scream and cry that he would do anything for Ruben to not let that happen. The other part of him wanted to be strong and tell him to piss off. His two sides clashed and always ended in a stalemate, leaving him at a status quo.

"The choice is yours, David. I'll let you think about it. Call me later."

The room suddenly became still until Carlos' hamster made a clicking noise, sounding like teeth grinding repeatedly. David remembered when Carlos first brought the hamster home. There's was a point made to tell David about all the sounds a hamster could make. He wanted David to know if the hamster was ever in distress. There was the squeaking noise that meant he was happy, hissing meant he was angry or threatened, and the clicking meant he was content and in the best of moods. David rolled his eyes at the information when Carlos told him and never thought he would ever think about it again.

He wondered what the hamster could be content about, sitting in a cage all day, eating and pooping in the same space. It certainly didn't sound like a cheerful spot, but then again, his world was contained in that space, having no clue what else existed outside his universe. To him, he was king of the hamster universe, which made David kind of envious of the hamster. His world was his with no care in the world, squeaking and clicking. David wondered what made the hamster happy. Finally, he fixated on his torch on the nightstand and closed his eyes, trying to let the images float away, unsuccessfully.

***

David awoke in the recliner suddenly from Carlos, slamming the front door.

"DAVID," yelled Carlos, half in a dream. David could barely make out Carlos, but could tell he was upset.

"When were you going to tell me?"

David's vision cleared, and he saw Carlos' forehead scrunched and his hands were on his waist. It was typical of Carlos to go full-blown accuser without having all sides of the story, even if David did not know what the problem was.

"What…What? What are you talking about now?"

David left the living room and escaped to his room. Slamming the door, he laid down on his unmade bed on top of a layer of unfolded clothes. Carlos followed him in.

"It's better if you come clean and admit to it. I can't help you if you deny everything. I'm giving you the chance to tell me what happened. Please don't lie."

"You're going to have to be more specific. I have zero clue what you're talking about."

Carlos was getting impatient. David felt trapped inside the room with him. Closed rooms always made David feel uneasy, but maybe Carlos, too, felt the same way and hoped he would move.

"Santos. Santos Morelo. Ring a bell?"

David's eyebrows raised, and he was now paying attention to him. "Do you know Pops, I mean Mr. Morelo?"

"Admit knowing him?"

"It's not a crime to know someone. What?"

"The man's dead."

"I know."

They both stayed quiet and avoided eye contact. "How do you know that?"

"Doesn't matter. I just do. I know it's sad because he was a good person."

"David, I can't give you the details, but someone murdered him and died of an overdose, and after an anonymous tip came in, we went back to the scene and found what he overdosed on."

"And?"

"And? And we found your fingerprints at the scene and all

over the house. The tip that came in also gave us details of how you swapped his pills for what killed him. Your prints were also on the pill container. To make matters worse, the neighbour saw you there several times, including the day of his murder. It doesn't look good."

"I don't know what to say. You really can't think I would do something like that. I mean, I'm not a murderer. I liked the guy."

"I know, little brother, but I have to do my job and bring you in, at least while we investigate these claims. In fact, I called a black and white over dispatch to meet me here. I will make sure he escorts you over to the precinct to ensure things are handled properly, you know, to avoid a conflict of interest. I want nothing getting fouled up on a technicality."

David hated hearing Carlos call him that. Little brother was something he called him when they were smaller, way before their parents had marital problems.

Back when they would still take family trips every summer.

Back when they were still a family.

David could perceive Carlos's genuine conflict and genuine remorse. David found himself literally backed into a corner.

"I understand, but Carlos, there's no way I did this. There *has* to be something else going on."

"Maybe, but for now, we got to go. I'll tell Moody not to cuff you until you arrive at the station, but let's move."

David noticed Carlos avoid eye contact with him. The disappointment written across his face made David wondered whether Carlos would truly treat him fairly and give him a chance to prove his innocence. Thinking there was no better way of showing this than cooperating with him and going in willingly, so he did. David sensed Carlos's guilt radiate from him, but surely Carlos would give him the benefit of the doubt, he thought. *David had to.*

David remembered the last thing their mother told Carlos before they moved to New Mexico was to watch over him and keep him out of trouble. Carlos failed on both counts because of David.

The questions would soon mount, and David secretly hoped he could keep his drug use quiet for as long as possible, but going into jail, he didn't know for how long he would be able to. David saw a police car pull up to the house and figured it was his ride.

"David, go with the officer. They know not to cuff you. I'll meet you at the precinct for processing, ok?"

"Alright, you'll be right behind?"

"Yes, David. Don't worry. We'll get through this."

The car ride was silent. At the station, they met Sergeant Moody at booking and processed David. Booking was unusually quiet. The authorities had transported everyone to the county earlier, and they were not holding any new individuals.

It left David to sit alone in holding, waiting for his fate to unfold. David didn't enjoy seeing his brother on the other side of a concrete holding cell. Sitting on a concrete bench, shoeless, and nervous again was not a fun time for David. Finally, their eyes met, and somehow, David saw Carlos was feeling almost as bad as he was. Before long, Carlos's phone beeped, and David assumed it was work dragging him away.

"Hey David, I gotta go check on stuff, but I shouldn't be long. I'll come back and check on you soon. If you need anything, just buzz, Moody. He's on duty, ok?"

"Thanks, it's kind of cold man and they took my shoes, and they didn't give me a blanket or anything."

"Dang, well, I'll let Moody know about the blanket, but

not much I can do about the cold, alright. Sorry. I'll be back. Try not to worry."

"Easier said than done, but thanks anyway."

From inside holding, David could get a glimpse of his brother sitting at his desk. If he pressed his ear to the door, where there were gaps in the seams, he could hear his brother speak. Occasionally, he would see Carlos glance back at him and smile back as he typed away almost manically until his phone beeped and he stopped to answer the phone. Moving toward the bottom of the door, where the gap was larger, David heard his brother's conversation better.

"Henry, I was going to," Carlos said, but not before being interrupted.

"I know. I haven't given you an update yet."

The conversation got muffled. David adjusted until he found a better listening spot.

"I can be there in twenty. See you then," Carlos said.

As the conversation ended, David moved upward toward the little viewing window. From its thick glass, Carlos waved back and motioned that he would be back. All David did was smile and wave back, hoping his case would take a turn for the better.

Henry's choice of location surprised Carlos when he arrived at Valley City Lake. Tourists and boaters mostly cluttered the lake, which was not a place where locals usually went. Then again, Henry wasn't exactly a local anymore.

At the top of the bank on a bench, he found him overlooking the fishing dock. The sun was still high in the sky. From behind, Henry seemed peaceful, and Carlos could tell he was deep in thought. Henry held his head back and gazed up into the clouds. The grass muted his arrival.

"Henry," Carlos said.

"I didn't hear you come up."

"How are you? I feel like it's been weeks since I saw you. I know I'm exaggerating, but it really feels like a long time."

"Thanks for coming. I'm glad to see you too. Sit."

Henry's smile always tickled Carlos in a certain way deep down inside and felt like lava coming out of his pores, forming a warm sensation that rose from his gut and to his neck. It made him miss being smiled at.

"You're probably wondering what's been going on with your father's case."

"I think that's obvious. I'm joking. Continue. Sorry. I lash out with humour when I'm nervous."

"I have some news."

Carlos still couldn't muster the strength to disclose to him his brother had been arrested as the prime suspect, nor how to spin the news. Carlos could see Henry's whole body shrink down as the anticipation of the news weighed down on him.

"We made an arrest."

It was very unusual for the ducks on the lake to come close to the shore because of the constant boats passing back and forth. The waves would cause them to nest somewhere else, but here they were. A large group of ducks had surrounded them and looked like they were begging for food. When they realized there was none to be given, they left as fast as they had appeared. The ducks had given the conversation a beat to breathe, but Henry was now expected an explanation and details.

"Let me just get it out before you ask questions."

"I'm listening."

"Remember, I told you our medical examiner had found rat poison in his system?"

Henry nodded.

"Okay, well, after further investigation, we found other drugs in his system, namely methamphetamine. That's what really caused his death, coupled with the lack of his heart medicine. It would seem he stopped taking his heart pills."

"My dad stopped taking his pills and somehow had meth in his system. How did this happen?"

Carlos moved a little closer to Henry and slowed his speech before speaking.

"We suspect the person we have in custody is involved in your father's death. We have evidence he replaced your father's pills with ones that look exactly like them, with one exception. They filled them with meth instead. We don't know exactly how he did it, just that we found his prints on the scene and a witness has placed him on the scene on the night of your father's death."

The ducks waded on the surface, dipping their heads in and out of the water. Many of the ducklings were grasping for their mother, trying to avoid being left behind. The mother duck then stopped and waited for all of them to catch up before they swam farther away to the other side of the shore toward home.

It reminded Carlos of how he used to follow his father around when he was a kid. There weren't that many happy memories with his father early on, but most of the happy ones involved Sunday church and lunch at Golden Corral, where he could stuff himself silly with brownies and chocolate-covered marshmallows.

Despite not being a big fan of church, the promise of unlimited munchies motivated him after an hour of good behaviour. In his opinion, the effort was valuable. It was the most time he ever got to spend with his father.

"This is a lot to take in, CJ, so who is this person who you have in custody?"

This was the question Carlos was dreading but knew was coming.

"As this is an ongoing investigation, I'm not at liberty to say just yet, but please trust me, I still have some more work to do. I have another suspect who might also be involved, but I haven't exactly turned the corner on it yet. I know you have been waiting patiently, so I just wanted to get you up to date where we stand at the moment."

"I think I'm going to need some time to process all of this. Do you mind if I head home, and we can talk about this later? I've still got my father's funeral to finish planning, and I think I just want to sleep it off."

"Of course. I totally understand. I have to get going myself," Carlos said.

Carlos hugged Henry and grasped the back of his head, giving him a peck on the cheek before leaving. Carlos really wanted to be honest and tell him their suspect was his brother, but every time he tried, his fear pushed the words back down. His brother's supposed involvement made him feel personally responsible somehow, and he didn't want to complicate things further, so he left that part out. The next time they met, he would need to tell him the truth.

His fear was that Henry would reject him, and someone blame him for his father's death. It would be hard to believe that living with his brother, that he never knew that something was "off."

Carlos spent so many hours at work dedicated to finding anyone in connection to their sister's death that he may have been blind to what was happening at home with his brother. Carlos lived with his brother and never saw the signs he was a meth addict. It didn't seem possible to him, but it was the truth. Maybe if Carlos was more observant of his home life, he could have avoided Henry's father's death. It was that fear which stopped him from telling Henry about his brother.

Flocks of birds landed on the edge of the water and were searching the grounds for food, pecking at the dirt, finding worms and other bugs to eat. Unfortunately, whenever they found something to eat, the waves from passing boats would scare them off, and their meal would escape them. This happened repeatedly. It would seem that they either didn't learn, or they didn't care about getting interrupted. Their single-mindedness in their task was something that Carlos could relate to.

It was his single-mindedness that allowed his brother to get in bed with whoever supplied him with the drugs and caused him to get himself into so much trouble. Carlos would repeat the previous days and months in his head for any clues to his brother's behaviour.

Other than his late nights and early mornings, he couldn't see much wrong. Meanwhile, he still didn't know how Ruben was involved in Santos' murder, but he sensed there was something more to it than he was seeing. Doubling down on Ruben would be Carlos' priority and hopefully see what else he could flesh out.

***

It was getting close to sundown. Earlier, when he did his preliminary research on Ruben, he got a list of his addresses and visited his home and see what activity he could observe. Despite the need for backup, he didn't call Moody or someone else and continued to ignore his captain's advice for backup and procedure because he couldn't afford to be wrong again. Like the ducks earlier, he felt as if he was grasping, but when you don't know any other way, it doesn't really feel like grasping. It seemed normal.

Carlos entered the address into his GPS; it took him to the far side of town, deep inside Treasure Hills. Treasure Hills was a kind of city inside of a city. Although technically part of Valley City, it had its own schools, parks, and even a library annex. Almost everything about Treasure Hills was just one step above Valley City. The streets were cleaner. The trees and lawns were well manicured. They did not allow any trashcans on the curb-side. The houses all shared a distinct style that didn't deviate from each other.

Arriving at the gatehouse, he flashed his badge to the guard, who let him in without question. Once the gates opened, a long palm-tree-lined driveway sprawled in front of him. On the right side, a nine-hole golf course stretched the full length of the neighbourhood. Each hole had exactly two sand traps and featured flags from different countries on each flagpole. It was the community's way of showing diversity when, in fact, Treasure Hills was anything but that.

Finding himself in such a place made Carlos wonder what their residents thought of him as he looked around and found no one that looked like him. In a city that was ninety-five percent Mexican American, it was strange to see so much White around him. Leave it to Treasure Hills to whitewash a brown community. Most of the houses were on the east side, and Treasure Hills' house design remained intact. Some were single story, but most were at least two.

Because of the unclear display of numbers, Carlos spent a minute finding Ruben's house. The housing association mandated integrating the numbers into the architecture of the homes to avoid any markings on the sidewalk, making it necessary to have a keen eye to find Ruben's home. At the end of the road near the cul-de-sac, he found it, parked two houses down, and waited.

Carlos wasn't sure what he expected to find outside Ruben's home, but he would not let any chance escape of tying him to Santos' murder. His visor pulled down, and he caught sight of his sister and David. They took the picture the summer before his sister was murdered.

Even now, years later, Carlos can still see the image of his sister spread across the ground, stabbed. It was something he tried to erase from his mind without success. Trying to ease the headache starting, he rubbed his temples and eyes. The buzzing of the streetlights jarred him back to reality where he realized hours had passed, and Carlos had observed no activity. Since it was a gated community, there was even less traffic than in a normal neighbourhood.

The only movement around him was the crickets that seemed to run the yards in packs. The stakeout at Ruben's home was a bust for now, so Carlos moved on to his backup plan, Ruben's shop. Leaving the gated community with no guard in sight, Carlos turned down onto Treasure Hills Boulevard and made his way down to Ruben's shop. The stark contrast between this part of town and the rest of Valley City astonished Carlos.

Compared to the rest of Valley City, the roads and homes in Treasure Hills were incredibly nice, surpassing the description of "pristine". The inequality was shocking to Carlos and no wonder Ruben made his home in this neighbourhood; it fit his M.O. Turning the corner after a few blocks, he saw the sign for Ruben's shop.

Outside of the graphic shop, he found the parking lot empty of cars. The front door had a closed sign, and most of the lights were off except for a single streetlamp flooding a pale-yellow hue onto the street. Bringing his flashlight, he parked his truck on the side street and exited, then shone his light on the windows and found nothing out of place. However, he noticed cameras positioned on the outer corners, facing the parking lot and the front door. They didn't seem to be on or moving, and since there was no visible light, he figured they were offline.

Moving to the back of the building, he found a vinyl padded door made of steel which was obviously made for keeping others out. Perhaps he had troubles in the past with burglaries, Carlos thought, but wouldn't he have mentioned that in his earlier interview with him?

There had to be another reason for that strong of a door to his business. It seemed unusual for such strong security in a graphics shop with no real merchandise to speak of other than clothes and printing supplies.

There didn't seem to be any cameras to speak of in the back area, which in itself was odd. None of it made sense to Carlos and just created more questions than it answered. Around the corner, he saw the Treasure Hills security officer pull up and approach him.

"Excuse me, sir, but what are you…"

Carlos pulled out his badge, cutting off the security officer.

"Sorry to bring you out here. I'm Detective Alvarado. I'm just following up on a case and checking the area for anything unusual."

"Did someone break into Mr. Delgado's?"

"No, no, nothing like that. Like I said, I was just following up on a lead," Carlos said as he turned off his flashlight and walked back toward his truck.

"Well, looks like nothing out of place here. I'll be on my way. Thank you, officer, for your help. Take care."

As Carlos sped away, he saw the confused expression of the security guard in his rearview mirror and hoped the guard wouldn't make a note of his being there.

18

CARLOS ARRIVED BACK AT THE STATION TO FIND another detective had pulled David from holding and was getting ready to question him. In the hallway, he found holding room two and peered into the window.

Inside, he saw his brother cuffed to the table alone and hadn't noticed Carlos at the door. With his eyes widening with each glance at his cuffs, David stared at his hands in disbelief, feeling defeated. He laid his head down on the table and closed his eyes.

Carlos wanted to go inside and tell his brother it would be alright, but it wasn't something he could have promised. His phone beeped a text message from Missy:

```
Detective, the info you
requested, Detective Salinas
and Ruben Delgado. Let me know
if this helps.
```

He immediately acknowledged the message and tried to hide his smile. Upon examining the clipboard on the door, he discovered Salinas was assigned to his questioning, which led him to believe that seeing Salinas' name again couldn't be a coincidence. Salinas normally handled petty crimes, burglary, and other financial crimes, but never murder cases, so it made him wonder how he got assigned to his brother's case. He found the captain's signature next to his name, proving he had signed off on it.

"Alvarado, what are you doing here?"

"I wanted to see who was questioning my brother."

"I think you better leave. You don't want people to think you are interfering in your brother's case."

"I'll stay and observe from the other side," Carlos said as he pointed over to the next room.

"I don't want you to be interrupting us. Just stay on your side, and we'll be fine." Salinas' wrinkles protruded more than usual.

Carlos entered the other room and saw his brother through the glass mirror, unaware he was being watched. The room had a solitary table, two chairs in the middle, and a water cooler in the corner. An out-of-date metal fan swept the room from above David's head, creating a metallic buzz that faintly echoed in the small space.

Salinas knocked on the door and entered the room. The room was practically empty except for one mirror opposite David, where, at the right angle, Carlos glimpsed at his brother's face. The lines on his forehead told the entire story. Salinas sat in front of him and offered him water.

"David, I'm Detective Salinas. I have some questions for you. It's to your benefit you answer my questions as honestly as possible, understood?"

"Yes, sir."

"Good. First, how would you describe your relationship with Santos Morelo?"

"You could say he was a friend."

"A friend?"

David nodded.

"How is it that a twenty-four-year-old kid becomes friends with a sixty-eight-year-old man? How does that work?"

The fan above David slowed to a snail's pace. He could sense someone peering into the room from the door. Salinas across from him tapped his pen on the table.

"We met when I was a server at Benny's. He was one of my customers."

"Benny's? The reason for your firing at Benny's, according to your former boss, was repeatedly missing shifts and stealing from the cash register."

"That's a lie. I admit to missing shifts but stealing money...never."

"Fine, let's sidebar that for now. So, you met Mr. Morelo at work, then what? How did you strike up a friendship?"

"He started talking about how he needed help with his lawn, and I mentioned my father owned a lawn care business in the past. I told him about having experience mowing lawns and stuff, and he offered me a job."

"He offered you work. Is that right?"

"That's what I said."

"So, it was more of a business relationship, would you say?"

"It started that way, but it changed."

"How?"

"The more time I spent over there, the conversations became longer and more personal. We just seemed to get along. To be honest, I think he just missed his children, and I reminded him of his kid."

"Is that right?"

David agreed.

Salinas opened the folder on the table and displayed pictures of the scene.

"You see this. Each of these number markers is places we

found your fingerprints at his residence, which includes the dining room, kitchen, and, most importantly, the bathroom cabinet. Specifically, his medicine bottles had your prints all over them."

Carlos stood at the other side of the glass and, for the first time, uneasy about his brother's future. What were his prints doing on Santos' medications? he thought.

"Of course they are."

"Explain yourself."

"Sometimes we were outside drinking lemonade after doing a job that he asked me to retrieve his medications for him."

"And how are we supposed to corroborate that? Our only witness to that is dead."

David sat silent, and his face remained unaffected.

"Putting that aside for now, how do you explain being there on the night of his death? We have a witness that puts you there."

"Earlier in the day, he had me clean his office of all the extra clutter. I left his place around noon. That was the last time I saw him."

"We have a witness that puts you there later, around 8:00 p.m. to 9:00 p.m., entering the back of the house and then leaving ten to fifteen minutes later the same way. Care to explain?"

"I think you have a blind witness because I was never there that late."

"If you weren't there, then where were you?"

From Carlos's point of view, he could see David's face reacting to the question. He seemed to contemplate an answer. Where had he been and why wouldn't he say? For a moment, it looked like he was about to say something, but then stopped himself short. The wrinkles on face tripled and angled down.

"I was at home alone."

"It doesn't look good for you, David. The prints, the witness, the opportunity and motive."

"What motive?"

"The thousands of dollars, of course."

"You're not making any sense. What money?"

"Mr. Morelo apparently didn't enjoy using a bank. He had thousands of dollars tucked away under his bed in a lockbox."

Salinas removed some pictures from the folder and displayed them in front of David. He cycled through the pictures one by one, showing money hidden in a lockbox. David's face lost all its colour.

"I did not know."

"I'm going to give you some time to think about how we are going to continue this conversation later. Someone will be in to take you back to holding, but when we talk next, I want different answers from you."

"Detective Salinas before I go, am I under arrest?"

From the other side of the two-way mirror, Carlos smirked because somewhere deep inside of David, he had been listening to him when he was lecturing him on his rights when being pulled over all those various times.

"No, Mr. Alvarado, we are simply holding you for questioning at the moment while we gather more information."

"I see, and how long have I been answering your questions so far, Detective?"

"Mr. Alvarado, I wouldn't be getting smart with me. And as far as your question, it's been less than 24 hours."

With a minor grin, David bowed his head in acceptance, showing he had finished talking and was ready to go back to holding. Then the detective escorted him out.

Carlos stood without a word to say. Salinas had laid it out almost poetically for David. The logic he placed in front of

David was inescapable. Salinas entered the room. Carlos knew there had to be more. There had to be a reason for David denying he knew Ruben. He needed to find out what it was.

"Alvarado, I hate to say it, but your brother is making it harder on himself the longer he claims his innocence."

"I'm sorry, Salinas. I did not know how seriously you took your job. You questioned him by the book. Clean and straight."

"Thanks, I think. I'm going to let him stew for a while in holding before I question him again. I'll keep you posted."

Salinas left, and Carlos found himself alone in the room again. The lights were dim, and he allowed himself to see David more clearly than he had before. His fingers tapped the edges of the desk repeatedly. He must be nervous and wondering what must be in store for him next.

His eyes tearing up reminded Carlos of when they were kids. The last time he saw him cry. Carlos had no idea what David's future held for him. He only knew there was more work to be done, and he was the only one who could do it.

19

David woke up next to someone urinating in the only toilet. Holding was barely large enough for four people and already felt too small for David. With his belly protruding further than seemed humanly possible and his stubby legs, the person had a comical combination.

Wearing a yellow stained white shirt that he hoped was mustard caught David's attention, but what stood out the most were his beady eyes that seemed to struggle to squint as if he couldn't see.

The man urinated, then faced David and winked at him as if they were long-lost friends who found each other after missing from each other's lives and then headed toward David but not before tripping on his shoeless feet, falling flat on his ass. Scooting himself to the nearest cement corner, the man placed his hands under his head and fell back asleep.

There was nothing for David to do but wait for them to press charges and formally arrest him and take him to prison. After all the trouble he had put him through, he really didn't know why he was protecting Ruben.

It was true Ruben always had a seemingly endless supply

of drugs, and David was always too weak to say no to crystal, especially if he wasn't paying for it.

Even though their relationship was mostly about drugs, there was always a part of him that felt something for him. It would have been difficult for him to have sex with him without feeling something. It's true the crystal did help, but somewhere deep down, hidden under the fog of meth, he cared for Ruben. But he wasn't too sure if Ruben felt the same for him. Every time he tried to bring up something serious to Ruben, Ruben would force-feed him a pipe and shelve the conversation.

None of that mattered, anyway. Soon, he would be feeling the effects of not smoking crystal. Last week, David tried his very hardest to keep track of all the stuff he smoked, writing 0.5 grams, a twenty, and so on in his little sticky pad he kept in his pocket.

At the end of the night, he counted it all up and found that he was smoking almost a quarter of an ounce. It was unbelievable, if he had paid for it, he would've had a 300-dollar-a-day habit.

It was no wonder he felt withdrawal effects after only two days. He hated to feel that way. The sweaty hands would come first, then the uncontrollable shakes and unbearable nausea, followed by the nightmares. David figured the only good thing about coming out of going to prison was his forced withdrawal. Going to prison was something he didn't want, but if he did, it would at least solve one of his problems.

The lights in the room dimmed, and a guard knocked at the metal door which slid open, throwing brown paper bags and juices at them.

David glanced at the clock outside in the hall; it was already 6:00 p.m. Dinner time.

David opened the brown bag and found two white bread sandwiches with a slice of bologna inside of them, two slices of cheese in plastic wrap, and packages of mayonnaise and mustard. Inside, he also found a small white Styrofoam cup filled with raisins. The drunk didn't wake up, and he wasn't about to tell him dinner came, so he carefully ate his dinner and chugged the juice box. Almost as soon as he had sat back down on the concrete ledge, his stomach growled, and not in the good way.

The trouble with withdrawal is you feel you need to throw up, but in actuality, you don't need to. It can become a horrible cycle of always feeling sick and not sick at the same time. The stomach cramps were real, but the vomit never came. It was so long since he had these feelings; he forgot eating solid foods always made it worse.

David tried laying down on one side, then the other, and finally settled on his back. Shooting pain, then nothing with a way to end it. Back home, he would have smoked some weed or popped a Xanax pill or two, but here there was nothing, so he would have to sit in this concrete box and suffer quietly.

Eventually, he passed out, but minutes later woke up the banging guard who silently walked him over to the interview room. There was no one around the hallways. It was eerily silent. The guard placed him in the room and locked it behind him. They didn't place cuffs on him, which he found strange while he sat in the only chair and waited, waiting for what was the question he should have asked himself. Another knock came at the door, and Salinas, the same detective from before, came in.

"Hello, David. I hope your time in holding and a meal has made you a bit more cooperative. How are you feeling?"

"Okay."

"That's it? Just okay, huh? I need you to take this seriously and be honest with me. I am only giving you one more chance to tell me the truth and explain yourself."

David kept his mouth closed and picked at his thumb, cleaning his nail.

"Nothing to say. Fine. You don't need to say anything. Just listen."

Salinas grabbed his phone and played a voice recorder for David to hear. It was a conversation with Salinas and another man. After listening to a couple of beats, David recognized the voice. It was Julio, the nurse who watched over him at the lake house. He then listened more closely while Salinas watched his every move. David leaned his head in closer to the phone on the table.

"Mr. Alfaro, I'm Detective Salinas. Do you know why you are here?"

"I'm not exactly sure. Have I done something wrong?"

"That all depends on what you consider wrong," said Salinas, who paused a few seconds. "Let me give you some facts. We came upon your house because we tracked a cell phone's location to it. The location started at a residence in Treasure Hills and then eventually made its way to your home. Any of this sound familiar?"

"Nothing? Okay, I'll continue. The phone's location didn't change for over twenty-four hours and then ended up at another residence in Valley City, where last night we arrested the individual for murder... are you sure there isn't anything you want to share with me?"

David empathized with Julio because he knew what it was like to be grilled by Salinas, but his empathy only went so far. Julio helped him, but only because Ruben forced him to. David wondered if Julio considered how stupid of a mistake it was to help Ruben. He hoped it would cost him his job.

Mesmerized by the audio recording, David almost forgot

where he was at. Salinas waited for him to say something, anything, yet David said nothing.

"Don't have to make it hard for yourself. Can you guess how Julio answered my question?"

"How?"

"You need to stop playing games. We know everything, okay? Julio admitted to having you at his place for over twenty-four hours, watching you after your near overdose, and he has confirmed that Ruben Delgado was the one providing the methamphetamine to you and him and countless others. You don't need to pretend anymore."

With the last statement, David's insides grumbled and caused him to hold his stomach in deep, piercing pains. His palms became sweaty, and a wave of nausea ran him over like a truck. It was almost impossible for him to sit still, and he fell over in his chair to the ground. The pain had become too unbearable.

Glaring up at Salinas, David couldn't speak, so he tried to use his eyes to communicate the need for help. Salinas stared back, unchanged. David realized how it must look to him, just someone trying to get out of answering questions by pretending to be sick, but he wasn't pretending.

David squirmed around for a few moments before he noticed Salinas radio a guard over helping him over to the infirmary. The guard grabbed David and held him up with his arms as he trudged him down the hall to the infirmary. David walked on his tippy toes with some effort, but still was in some considerable pain. He was glad the guard was not giving him any grief for the help to the infirmary, where he hoped he would get some help.

While being escorted to the infirmary, David noticed his brother sitting on the far side of the station from the corner of his eye. The volume of his voice failed to register anything audible. David didn't want to be alone in the infirmary, but what choice would he have? As he entered the room, Carlos left his desk.

Inside the infirmary, David found it to be empty, minus an old man cobbled in the corner with an IV drip in his arm, asleep. As they dragged him onto a gurney, David's vision was failing, and the doctor mumbled something about dehydration while checking his vitals.

A wave of cold liquid rushed through him as he got an IV drip of his own. The doctor mouthed something, but David only made out the word saline. As he closed his eyes, he heard chatter all around him between a guard and the doctor. Focusing on the background, he heard Carlos arguing with Salinas somewhere outside.

"What the hell. You were supposed to call me when you started up again. What happened? Where's my brother?"

"David is in the infirmary. He's fine."

"What? Why?"

"I don't know. The guy just collapsed in pain, holding his stomach. They are looking him over now."

"Salinas, you're a real asshole."

Around the corner, a guard escorting David back into the interview room showed up. The guard brought him through the rows of desks eventually to the hallway where Carlos and Salinas stood. David was holding his stomach and slowly limped his way closer.

"David, are you alright? What happened?"

"It's okay. It's silly. Two days have passed since I last had any stuff in my system. I'm used to this happening. The withdrawals are killer. Every time I say they are going to be not as bad, but every time they are worse. I guess it's my penance."

"Don't say that, David. But is there anything we can do to make you feel better?"

"I just gotta push through it."

"Enough. We need to finish our interview. Alvarado, I'm going to need you to leave the interview room."

David sat down in the chair from earlier but, this time, knowing his brother was on the other side of the mirror, gave him some comfort, and he quickly nodded in the general direction of where Carlos might be.

"David, now I need you to respond to the information you heard. What do you say?"

David thought about how he could get himself out of the trouble he was in. They seemed to want to connect Ruben with the drugs, but there was no mention of how all this related to Santos' death. He still did not know what would happen if he gave up Ruben.

"You asked me earlier how I could prove I wasn't the one who killed Mr. Morelo, right?"

Salinas flicked his hand to hurry up.

"I told you I was home alone, and I had no alibi, but that wasn't true. I wasn't home. The entire night and the following morning, I was with Ruben, partying and getting high. There."

David relaxed, slouching his shoulders down in the chair with his hands flat on the table. His eyes directed at Salinas, no longer avoiding him.

"Wait, let's back up. So, you admit to knowing Ruben Delgado?"

"Yes."

"And Julio Alfaro, you know him too and spent the night at his place?"

"Yes."

"And what about the drugs? Who supplied them?"

"Ruben."

"You understand that all of this information will be double-checked and verified. Why are you now being so cooperative?"

"I wanted to protect Ruben, but I realized he's never really cared about me. It was always about what he wanted out of me. I'm just sad it took all of this for me to realize it. I really did care for him, but I guess I was just fooling myself. Plus, I'm willing to do whatever it takes to prove to you I wasn't at Santos' house when he was killed."

"You know we will have to bring in Mr. Delgado to get his side of the story. I hope it matches up, for your sake."

Salinas knocked on the door and had the guard take him back to holding. A few seconds after, Carlos exited the other side of the room and looked in astonishment at Salinas. Was his brother telling him the truth? He wondered.

To see what Ruben's side of the story was, he would have to wait. Salinas and he exchanged glances. Then he was out the door to bring Ruben in for questioning.

Hoping that something would finally stick to Ruben because it was David's only chance at survival.

20

CARLOS WASTED NO TIME LEAVING, ALMOST LEAPING outside of the interview room. Before he could exit, Salinas beat him down the hallway.

Unaware he was being watched; Salinas manically typed at his computer. Carlos couldn't see what he was doing, but whatever it was, it seemed urgent and even from his point of view, Carlos saw the sweat pouring from Salinas.

The clicks of the mouse were so loud, even from a distance, it surprised Carlos. A new window popped up on his screen and Salinas haphazardly typed his message. After a few more clicks, Salinas closed the windows and turned off the monitor and looked around the room before speeding out toward the break-room.

Whatever had just happened, Carlos knew it couldn't have been good, so he left the station and rushed toward Treasure Hills.

CARLOS, ON ROUTE TO RUBEN'S BUSINESS, ASKED himself if his brother was telling the truth or simply lied to get himself out of trouble. David didn't always have the best track record for telling the truth. When they were kids, before things turned to shit between his parents, they went camping at Gardner State Park. They opted to rent a cabin instead of using a tent. The cabin had dirt floors, which made it feel like a tent. The only amenities were that someone had locked the door.

Given the state of things, David and his brother went out and explore the park and found the gooseneck waterfall. As they made their trip more inland to the park, they saw a sign that said: NO FOOD/WATER BEYOND THIS POINT. Carlos figured it would be a good idea to grab some water since they did not know how long until they arrived at the waterfall. Searching for money, he forgot to bring his wallet. In the excitement of leaving the cabin, he simply forgot about it.

After breaking the news to his brother, they found a plastic bottle in the trash and filled it with water from the bathroom. While Carlos filled the bottle, David took off around the corner to people watch. Carlos saw a mix of people and families that were on similar hikes like themselves, nodding as they all passed him. Finishing two bottles of water, he wondered what had happened to David, as he didn't seem to be anywhere around. Poking around the watering station and behind some other picnic tables, he saw him near the snack bar.

David was in line and purchasing something, but with what money? Later, when he asked about the money, David said he found it near the trashcan but wasn't sure if he was telling the truth.

Things like that always happened with David. The guy constantly lied about everything and sometimes simply for the fun of lying. When Carlos confronted him about his weed smoking, his brother flat-out lied about it, denied it and called Carlos a liar when, in fact, he smoked weed.

From the combination of the smells in his room, to the used packs of zigzags, and the constant clogs in his sink from bong water, Carlos was the one responsible for cleaning. There was no reason for David to deny it, and in fact, Carlos told him it was okay to smoke in his room. Carlos just wanted to hear from him he was smoking but he still denied it, and after a while, Carlos just dropped it. It was easier to just move on.

Carlos always found it difficult to believe his brother immediately. This time, though, he thought he might tell the truth, since his life might be on the line. Still, it would be his word against Ruben's, and for now, David wasn't exactly a stellar judge of character.

As he approached Treasure Hills, the lights flickered on. The streets were cleaner, the lawns more manicured, and the lights turned a shade whiter than the yellow that cast a stale hue over the rest of the city. It became very clear where one neighbourhood ended and another began.

Treasure Hill's homeowners' association opted to buy high-pressure sodium lamps that produced a whiter light and less maintenance overall. It hadn't dawned on Carlos that Treasure Hills' lights made everything seem whiter, even his dark-coloured truck. The neighbourhood screamed white.

As he approached the graphics shop, there seemed to be a few customers parked out front, so he parked near the rear, where he saw the massive steel door earlier, and waited for the customers to thin out. Carlos never questioned himself about doing the right thing or if a suspect was being detained for the right reason. He always felt that he was in the right and just in doing the work he did.

There was something different about Ruben.

Carlos felt it in his gut that something was off, but he couldn't put his finger on it. He was certain Ruben was shady and almost certainly caused his brother to overdose. How David and Ruben developed a relationship was beyond him.

Carlos knew he forced Julio to care for David instead of taking him to the hospital. His brother was lucky to survive. None of the facts connected him to Santos' death, so all he could do was continue to unravel the string and see where it led.

Instead of coming in from the front, he knocked from the back. Moments passed, as he heard several locks being removed before the steel door opened and Ruben came face to face with Carlos. Ruben's face didn't seem all that surprised and, in fact, had a smirk on it.

"Detective, entering from the rear, eh?"

"No time for jokes, Mr. Delgado. I'm here to bring you in for questioning, but first, I'd like to have a look around your place of business, if you don't mind. Legally you can say no, but may I search your property?"

"Of course, Detective, anything I can do to cooperate. Please, come in. I was just closing up and drawing down the machines."

Carlos found it odd someone with something to hide, especially drugs, would openly invite the police to search without a warrant. If he had something to hide, it most certainly wouldn't be inside his business.

Inside he saw Ruben was indeed turning off his direct to garment machines which were making a low humming as powered off. Near the front door, Carlos noticed piles of boxes labeled baseball surplus with pictures of baseball gloves on them, given Ruben was involved in charity work with the softball team. Carlos assumed that's what they used them for or would use them for in the upcoming season.

After a careful search, Carlos found nothing unusual or out of place.

"Did you find what you were looking for?"

Carlos wasn't sure how to answer the question, so he did the only thing he could do: ignore it.

"Mr. Delgado, I appreciate your cooperation, but for now, we need to ask you some questions at the station. Would you mind following me over? I promise it won't take much of your time."

"Of course, after you."

After Ruben locked the front door and turned off the lights, he followed Carlos out the back door and exited the building. Carlos waited for Ruben to get into his car and then headed toward the station with Ruben in tow.

Keeping a close eye on him, he half expected Ruben to pull away and attempt an escape, but it never happened. Ruben seemed totally at ease, which made Carlos even more nervous and suspicious than before. It made him wonder how someone with so much to hide could act so casual—was Carlos wrong about him?

There was no way David was lying. He needed to find the missing piece to protect his brother.

Arriving at the station, they both walked in and approached the information desk and asked the duty officer to buzz them into the back. Through the doors, it was a left or right turn. Left would take them to holding, and right would take them to the detective's section and the interview rooms.

Without batting an eye, Ruben pointed right and walked in that direction. Carlos found it unusual that Ruben seemed to know his way around the station. He didn't mention it to him and kept watching him closely instead.

The pair encountered Salinas in the interview room where David faced questioning.

"Ah, Alvarado, good job. This must be Mr. Delgado. I'm Detective Salinas, and I will handle your interview."

"Good to meet you, Detective. Whatever I can do to help."

The two of them paused for a moment and locked eyes. They spoke no words and made no facial expressions. Their entire bodies lacked any movement. Carlos was always a student of body language. The two of them displaying none was telling. Lack of body language is, in fact, body language. Unsure of what it meant yet, but he could tell a conversation was being held, even if he wasn't a part of it yet.

Salinas escorted him into the room, and Carlos took his place on the other side of the room across from the mirror. Carlos knew Ruben had no way of explaining himself out of the mess that Salinas was about to lay into him.

Having his brother cleared of all charges is what he was about to do, so it could be all over and they could go back to rebuilding their relationship. Most of all, he wanted Ruben to pay for getting David hooked on meth. David was in enough trouble without adding drugs to his list.

"Will you please state your name for the record?"

"Ruben Benavides Delgado."

"Do you know the reason for bringing you in today?" Ruben sat and looked around the room until his gaze stopped at the two-way mirror. His eyes deepened, as if straining to see through the mirror. His smile slowly grew to a disproportionate size for his face. It made Carlos think of Pennywise, the clown in one of his favourite Stephen King novels.

Carlos averted his eyes and knew he wasn't staring at him directly, but it made him feel uncomfortable. There was something oddly familiar and sickening about his smile.

"Mr. Delgado, I would appreciate you taking this interview a bit more seriously. I need you to answer my question."

Ruben's demeanour changed and scooted his chair up and stood almost at attention, placing his hands on the table and interlocking his fingers.

"My apologies. I have no idea what this is about."

"Okay. Let me begin with this. Do you know someone by the name of Julio Alfaro, an ER nurse at Valley City Medical Center?"

Ruben tapped his fingers on the table and pointed his eyes upward as if he was thinking about the question. To Carlos, it seemed he was just stalling for time, trying to think of a lie. It was something he saw many times.

"The name doesn't ring a bell."

"The man seems to know you and claims to have purchased methamphetamine from you frequently and claims you threatened to expose his habits to his employers for things you needed him to do. For example, you had him care for your boyfriend, David Alvarado, after a terrible experience with PCP. Any of this sound familiar?"

This was the exact moment Carlos was waiting for. Ruben found himself backed into a corner with nowhere to go. There was no way he could deny or talk his way out of this. Carlos could almost hear the cuffs being slammed onto his wrists.

"No."

"No, to what?"

"Just no. No to knowing the individual. No to selling drugs. No to having a boyfriend. Yuck, no way. And No to anything sounding familiar. Just no."

"Are you certain of this? Because we have two people saying that they know you, including David Alvarado," asked Salinas.

"Alvarado? Wait a second. Alvarado, as in Detective Alvarado? Are they related?"

"You didn't know they were brothers?"

"How would I? I've never met this David or Julio Alfaro before. Are you sure this isn't some kind of game Detective Alvarado is playing with me? The detective has been stalking my place of business and home for the last week or so and even showed up at my business after I closed last night, skulking around the back. Security found him and couldn't explain his presence, and he bolted. It's all logged. How do I know this detective doesn't have some personal grudge against me?"

Carlos paced the room, kicking the floor and scuffing it with his shoes. He furrowed his brow, picking up the metal chair in the room and slamming it down. Lucky for him, the room was soundproof.

"The guy's like a ghost. One second, he's not around, and then BOOM, he pops up out of nowhere, just like the Fair Park Slasher, flashing his badge around. I'm not the one with the problem. He is. You know, people always thought the Fair Park Slasher was a cop or someone with inside knowledge."

Carlos tried so hard to stomach it back down, to not think about it because he wanted it to be over so badly, putting it to the back of his mind, the Fair Park Slasher. Why would Ruben mention it?

He had to be playing with him, trying for a reaction. Creeping closer to the glass, he came face to face with it and listened. Hearing the ticking clock over Ruben's snickering caused Carlos to break.

At first, Carlos tapped the glass with his head slowly, and as the seconds grew, his intensity increased; it took everything he had to stop himself from smashing his head through the window—or hurting himself trying.

Suddenly stopping, thinking of David's emotional state,

Carlos wondered if his brother was going to help him or not. Strength is what David needed the most from Carlos. Luckily Salinas and Ruben hadn't heard his tapping in the mirror. The situation still left him angry, wanting to ask Ruben more questions, but they would have to wait.

"Mr. Delgado, I understand you are frustrated, but accusing a detective of stalking is not something we take lightly. Do you even have proof of this?"

"I gave our security firm, who handles both my home and business, pictures and videos I took frequently. I had them hold them in case the situation escalated, to which it obviously has."

"I, see. I promise we will take your concerns seriously, but right now I need to know where you were on March twelfth between 8:00 p.m. and 9:00 p.m."

Ruben's smile turned to a smirk and shook his head and turned his attention again to the two-way mirror.

"Very specific. Let me see, I was at the office working late. There was a large order of posters to fill before the morning."

"Can anyone vouch for your whereabouts?"

"An officer was there that night. I saw him when I arrived and when I left. He even patrolled by my office around that time. You can call them and confirm this."

"Very well. I will need their name and address and any contact information you have. But for now, an officer will escort you to our break-room, where you can have some coffee and a snack if you wish while we investigate your claim."

"Thank you."

Carlos watched as they were escorted out and then raced inside the room, throwing the door open out of breath. Treating big donors to the department like they were special was something he hated, especially when they gave them free fun of the building.

It would seem all it took was some free baseball uniforms and good will to the community to get a place at the table. Salinas, alone in the room, made notes while the lights dimmed in the room, causing the two-way mirror to become visible and was startled by Carlos's entrance, causing his pen to scribble off the paper.

"Salinas. Don't tell me you believe him. The guy is obviously lying."

"Alvarado. Stop. It is our job to investigate and take any accusations seriously. Do you understand?"

Carlos' right eye was beginning to eek a twitch, and his voice seemed to break with every other word.

"But there's no way that he is telling the truth. Stalker? Come on!"

"It sucks to have accusations thrown at you, but I will sort this out. You've got to give me time on this. Can you please chill while I look into this?"

"Fine. But the second you hear anything, you let me know. Not like last time. Got it?"

"I got it. Now go to your office and just try to relax. I'll come get you when I know more. Now, go, please."

Carlos tapped him on the back, then walked by the break-room and saw Ruben eating donuts and coffee, chatting with one of the other officers. Ruben was smiling and eating his donuts and his coffee and didn't seem to have a care in the world. Carlos wondered why everyone always seemed to get along with the man.

Back at this his desk, he had no other choice but to wait around, so he began reading the background reports on Ruben again, trying to find something, if anything, that didn't match up with the story. Carlos still couldn't get Ruben's words out of his head. *Fair Park Slasher. Fair Park Slasher.*

It wasn't like the phrase was the most common thing to

say. Ruben couldn't have known how it would have made Carlos react. There was no way Ruben would have known what happened to his sister. It reminded him of the card he saw at Santos' house. All this time investigating and didn't come up with one shred of evidence that the Fair Park Slasher was involved. It truly was like he was a ghost.

Carlos could find no connection. It had to be a coincidence, but Carlos didn't like to believe in them and for now, he had more important things to worry about than the Fair Park Slasher. His brother's life was on the line.

Carlos began scrolling through the pages again, read over the same information, and came to the same conclusion.

Nothing stuck out.

Ruben seemed clean.

Carlos then searched through his old files on the Fair Park Slasher. There were five murders, including his sisters. All of them were female and under the age of nineteen. They all were home alone and left for dead somewhere outside of their home. Trails of blood led from their homes to the outside, where their bodies were discovered with fatal stab wounds.

Investigators found no clues, DNA, or evidence of any kind. There were no witnesses. The only commonality was the card left behind at the scene with the park logo and the small traces of meth found on the card. After his sister, the murders suddenly stopped, and the case went cold. He was searching for clues ever since. Carlos scoured the new reports and internet for any sign of his sister's killer, but nothing ever came up. The case went cold.

Carlos didn't even know why he still harassed speed dealers about it. They always gave him the '*What the fuck you talking about face*' when he asked them about it.

First chance he got, he wanted to ask Ruben about his phrasing earlier but not before he confronted him about the stalking allegation. Carlos went to his place of business and home, but stalking was exaggerating and really had only spent a few hours at each place, and nothing came of it, so he didn't feel the need to divulge that information to anyone.

From around the corner, he heard a whistle in his direction. It was Salinas calling him over, so he locked his computer and headed back to the hallway down to the interview room. Once there, he found Salinas, Ruben, and Captain Rankin. It didn't look good.

"Captain, hey. What you are doing here?"

Rankin's face told the entire story. His eyes tilted down, and his posture hunched over. He seemed disappointed.

"Alvarado. Listen to what Salinas has to say, please."

Carlos turned to Salinas and waited for him to speak.

"Not sure how to say this, so I'll just say it. We called the security firm that handles the security tapes for his business and his home. On the night in question, we confirmed Mr. Delgado was at his place of business, working from 5:00 p.m. to around 11:45 p.m., at which time he arrived home at 12:05 a.m. and never left his till the next morning. The guy had no visitors and never left."

"What?"

"Your brother was lying when he said he was with Ruben on the night of Mr. Morelos' murder. And on top of that, we investigated Mr. Delgado's accusations of stalking. The security firm offered us the video files of his home and business security feeds. I know I don't need to give you all the details, but it sufficed to say we found evidence placing you at both locations on multiple days for several hours at a time. There was even an encounter with a security officer at his business on a night when Mr. Delgado wasn't even at work. The officer corroborated this on the scene. Mr. Delgado has more than enough evidence to press charges and ask for a restraining order."

Carlos' colour left his face, and there were no words to convey what he was thinking. Nothing he could say would make it right, so instead, he said nothing and kept thinking that Ruben must have squirrelled the security firm into his pocket somehow. Carlos wanted to believe his brother, but the evidence pointed against his word. Something must be missing.

"But surprisingly, Mr. Delgado has graciously agreed not to press charges and to look at the matter as a terrible lapse in judgment on your part, Carlos. Mr. Delgado understands that you have been under a lot of stress with what's going on with your brother, and your caseload has been heavy these past weeks. Since he is a friend of the force, he agreed to let the matter go. Isn't that big of him?"

"Gracious? Lapse in judgment? Who the FUCK."

Before he could finish, Rankin interrupted him.

"Alvarado. That's enough. Get out of here. Go to your office, home, I don't care where. Just get out of here now. Not another word. Go!"

Carlos glared at Ruben, wanting to say more, but his eyes would have to communicate his hate and distrust. He wanted to crack his head in and watch the blood spill on the pristine tiled floor, but didn't. Carlos needed to think of his brother, so he walked away. Before he crossed the corner, he saw Ruben shaking hands with Rankin and Salinas as they escorted him out of the station.

They were letting him go.

Now everything squarely fell on David. It was only a matter of time before Salinas and Rankin filed official charges against David now that his 48 hours were rapidly approaching, and the evidence was quickly piling up against him.

Since Ruben denied being with David or even knowing him and had no alibi for his whereabouts on that night; he hoped his brother would tell him the truth about what really happened because he couldn't think of anything else to get him out of this mess.

Tomorrow would prove challenging. Carlos headed home, hoping inspiration would come to him on what to do because otherwise, he believed his brother would be in a difficult situation.

21

THE NIGHT WAS LONG FOR CARLOS, TOSSING AND turning and only sleeping for stretches of an hour at times. Every time he woke, he panicked and almost forgot for an instant his brother was behind bars. As fast as the reprieve was, his anxiety overwhelmed him almost instantly. The words of his parents kept ringing in his head: *Watch out for your brother, take care of him. He's your responsibility.* Carlos would try to go back to sleep, but the cycle would start over.

Finally, out of exhaustion, he passed out only to be woken by a voicemail alert the next morning on his phone that he didn't hear go off. The pale shades made no dent in the sun peeking through his window. Squinting at the phone, he pushed the voicemail icon and played it on speaker.

"Hey, CJ, it's Henry. I rarely do this, but since you didn't answer the first three times, I thought it would be best to leave you a voicemail for when you woke up. I called because I was wondering if you might or if you want to come over and help me sort through some of my dad's stuff. I have to find something for the funeral for him and see if there wasn't

anything of value in his room. I mean, no pressure, but if you want and if you're free, then call me back. Okay, okay, bye."

It was a long time since Henry left a message for him on his phone. It was strange hearing his recorded voice. Carlos could hear the inflections and lack of inflections in his speech, how he would emphasize words like *wondering* or *pressure* or even *if you want.*

It made Carlos smile for the first time since the entire ordeal with his brother began. His curtain was no longer protecting him from the sun, so he shook it open to let the rest of the sunshine in, bathing in the yellow and causing his skin to tingle. Seeing as the timestamp on the voicemail was two hours old, he got himself up and quickly dressed to make his way over to Henry's.

Exiting his bedroom into the living room, he heard a loud scratching and squeaking noise. Mr. Hamster, he had never gotten around to naming him, was probably hungry. Since David wasn't home, he probably was neglected for some time, so he grabbed the food from the pantry and poured some into his food bowl. The little monster devoured the treat and seemed content.

Before leaving, he walked into David's room, deciding on whether he should clean it. Scattered clothes, a cracked bong on the floor, and the same stench of weed and patchouli incense permeated the room. No matter where he was, whenever he smelled that incense, he always would think of his brother. While he was sleeping, he kept thinking about his brother sitting alone in that holding cell on those concrete slabs, in the death grip of withdrawal, waiting for the unknown.

Carlos did his research, and Ruben still seemed to be outside of his grasp. If he hadn't gone home last night, he probably would have made a mistake and done something he would have regretted. His gut told him somehow Ruben's involvement was more than he or Salinas could prove.

Each time he thought he made progress; someone would abruptly close another door in his face. It made his stomach turn to think Ruben could go home without recourse. The only way to help his brother was to keep his cool and remain close to the case.

In the corner of David's room near his high school yearbook, a picture of David and him at the *My Chemical Romance* concert at Emo's in Austin stuck out. The aging picture he hadn't seen in ages with his red hair streaks and slim jeans made him smile. Carlos remembered how close he and David were and would do anything to get that closeness back. Tucking the picture back, he made a promise to himself he would help, somehow.

The only way that could happen would be·the evidence he collected against Ruben, and any would be accomplice be by the book and exact. Carlos knew down the line he might need a warrant and didn't want to be caught with his proverbial pants down, so he had Judge Romero's number saved and on standby in case he needed it. The judge helped him out in the past and never balked at him whenever he called at odd hours for warrants as long as they were justified and the paperwork in order, which is what he planned to do.

THE DRIVE OVER TO HENRY'S WAS QUIET. ALONG the way, Carlos passed remnants of the old Valley City Ice Plant that had been closed for over forty years. Its walls had holes punched into it and dotted the structure up and down its spine. Carlos pulled onto Wichita Boulevard, which took him down to Basin Circle, where Henry lived.

There was no way he could avoid passing the Valley City

Police Station. Back when Carlos just arrived on the force, they moved the station to where it stands now, making it only a few years old.

The city council deemed it cheaper to demolish the former location because of black mold, rather than repair it. The neighbourhood of Fair Park where Henry lived was always a quiet neighbourhood, but as the station moved in, things got worse. Vandalism grew, and the "safe area" became less safe.

There was a local baseball stadium that, in its prime, was home to the Valley City Roadrunners, a minor league baseball team. Only two years after the station moved, the walls crumbled, and the team moved cities. Carlos could never understand how the introduction of a police station in a neighbourhood increased crime.

When he arrived at Henry's, he found him outside in the front yard, piling stuff up into his father's old truck. Carlos honked his horn and flagged him down.

"Hope I'm not too late," asked Carlos.

"Perfect timing. I need your help to move the table from the kitchen. Do you mind?"

Carlos followed him inside the house, where he noticed Henry packed things up and marking their contents. Henry looked like he was pretty busy all morning, since most of the house seemed packed away.

"Here, I'll grab this side. You grab the other."

The table must have been solid wood, because it weighed more than it looked. Meanwhile, the sweat on his brow became so obvious, Henry gave Carlos a break.

"It's probably early for you on a Saturday, but don't tell me you're worn out already," said Henry.

"I'm fine. I just didn't expect it to be this heavy, besides I've got good stamina, or don't you remember?"

Carlos saw that maybe his joke went too far because Henry's face turned the colour of a ripe watermelon.

"CJ, be careful there. If I didn't know any better, I'd think you were flirting with me," said Henry with the slyest of grins.

"Well, maybe I was," winked Carlos.

They continued on to the outside, where they stopped on the lawn.

"You can put it down, CJ. Let's leave it here. Help me with my father's room. I saved it for last."

"Henry, if you don't mind me asking, what are you doing with all this stuff?"

"I wasn't sure at first, but I think most of it I am going to donate to the Valley City Catholic Diocese. My dad went to church every Sunday, so I figured it would be fitting. I spoke to Father Rob, and he agreed to speak at the funeral, so that's good."

"Makes sense. I'm glad you're doing something charitable with the stuff you don't need."

Carlos stood there watching Henry. So many years passed, and yet here he was still feeling the same way. There were only two people his entire life that really got him: his sister, and Henry. For a while, he lost both, and now Henry was sort of back in the picture.

"CJ. You alright? You kind of zoned out for a second."

"I'm sorry. I got lost in thought."

"Is there something on your mind? Wait, don't answer that. Of course, there is. You still must be worried about my father's case. You said that you had some other lead to investigate still? How's that going?"

Carlos found himself again unsure of what to share with him. It always seemed like there was one more piece of evidence that he needed to share with Henry. Just one more piece that he didn't tell him. Carlos had no clue how to tell him the person currently in holding for his father's murder was his own brother.

Whenever he thought of it, his heart raced, and the words

just seemed to vanish from his lips. Now confronted with the question, he figured he couldn't delay it any longer. Without preparation, he blurted out the truth in rapid succession.

"I told you we arrested someone for your father's murder. That was true. I didn't tell you who that was. It was my brother."

Henry's face stilled as if all feelings slid off his face and onto the ground. Carlos' emotions went from zero to a hundred and waited for the hammer to fall on him from Henry but all he got silence minus the *chk-chk-chk-chk* sound of the sprinkler outside near the bedroom window which only made the silence more deafening for Carlos.

"I know, I know. I'm sorry I didn't tell you before. I just didn't want you to see me any differently. I didn't want you to think I wasn't working hard on your case for you. I also needed time to prove my brother's innocence. There. There it is."

"Your brother David did this? To my father," asked Henry.

"The evidence points to him, but I'm still working another angle. I still have time. David has a boyfriend who has gotten him all caught up in this mess and even addicted to meth, so trust me, there is more going on. I need a little more time. Please, you've got to understand."

Henry stood silent for a moment, as if considering his options. Eventually, he pointed to the house and asked Carlos to follow him into his father's bedroom.

"CJ, sit. Please."

To Carlos, it was like going to get reprimanded, but he didn't know why. The room lacked any natural sunlight and felt claustrophobic to Carlos. Not knowing what Henry was going to say made Carlos' pulse race. His heart felt like it was inside his throat.

"I get where you are coming from, but it needs to be clear

that your dishonesty gave me a not-so-pleasant flashback. Not to rehash the past, but please do not keep anything from me again. Okay?"

"Of course. I understand."

"Good. So, first things first," calmly said Henry as he grabbed the nearest thing within his grasp, which happen to be the side table lamp, and tossed it down to the ground, smashing it to a thousand pieces.

"Jesus Henry, what are you doing?"

"I needed to take my frustration out on something and I rather it be on the lamp than on you. Don't get me wrong, I'm still really pissed at you about this. You know how hard it is for me to trust people and especially with our history, you should know better."

Carlos knew there was nothing he could say to make it better, so instead of being eloquent, he just acknowledged his fault.

"You're right and I know. I can only try to do better. I am sorry, Henry."

"Don't apologize, just do better. Now, what are you going to do about your brother? Do you have anything on his boyfriend that could clear his name?"

"Other than a strong hunch, not exactly. We had him in custody last night, but he had an alibi for the time of your father's time of death. My captain let him go. He's probably back at home laughing it up."

"That's terrible. For your brother's sake, I hope you prove he's not the one who killed my father. I still don't understand why anyone would do this, anyway. Makes no sense."

"I know. I will not stop working till I do. You have my word."

With that done, Henry opened the closet door and revealed stacks of baseball gear that were piling up over the years. There were shirts, pants, pitching gloves, and boxes of baseballs. All the items that any coach would need.

"This is where I need your help. Help me sort through this, please," asked Henry.

Carlos sensed the shift in emotion in the air, but didn't want to push Henry any further; wanting to make his life easier, not harder, so he uncomfortably let the topic change.

In the dim closet light, one box stood out with a flap that seemed worn down.

"Henry, there isn't a light in here?"

Henry looked toward the entrance of the room and found no other switch.

"Hmm, guess not. Here."

Henry opened the curtains on the only window in the room and flooded the room with the mid-morning light.

"Ah. Thanks. Much better. Look at this. It doesn't seem to be coaching supplies. It's unmarked."

Carlos lifted the box and placed it on the bed, where they both could see its contents. Inside, they found old notebooks that had scribbles of dates and names with dollar amounts attached to them. It reminded Carlos of the notebook he found when he first investigated the property. Something to do with Santos' illegal bookie activity. Underneath the notebooks, inside a black and white composition book, they found a set of photos. From his vantage point, Carlos could not see what Henry found, only that he visibly gasped at his finding.

"What is it?"

"I don't believe it. It's a baby picture of me and my parents at one of those old Sears photo studios they used to have. My dad kept it all this time?"

Henry flipped through the pictures and removed the baby picture from the plastic covering holding it. It had faded to a brown shade years ago.

"Oh my god, look at me. I'm practically bald in this picture. I wonder how old I was?"

Carlos placed his hand out to Henry.

"Do you mind?"

Henry handed the photo over, and as Carlos glanced over it and saw Henry's parents' smiles, a somberness overcame him. Carlos couldn't remember the last time he saw his own parents smiling at each other, if ever. Happy for Henry and not wanting to ruin his moment, he pushed the feeling back.

"Henry. You looked so tiny and cute! Both of your parents looked so happy."

"Stop it. You're gonna make me blush."

Henry continued to dig through the box and found several Dallas Cowboy jerseys and a matching cap, pausing when finding those items.

"Henry, what's the matter?"

Henry smacked his lips and brushed his hair out of his face. His eyes refocused and continued to gaze at the jerseys.

"I don't know if you remember, but my father was a huge Cowboys fan. Every weekend when they played, he would get into his getup, park himself in front of the TV, put on the game, and quietly and methodically watch. He would scribble into his little notebook, making notes about who knows what. Like clockwork. He never missed a game."

Henry picked up the jerseys and cap.

"My dad would wear these. These exact ones. I remember because he would rotate the only two jerseys he had and use the same hat."

Carlos sat down next to Henry on the bed and placed his arm around him. The bed sank in and squeaked as he moved closer to Henry. The sunlight from the window reflected off the dresser mirror and back into Carlos's eyes. Henry continued to stare at his father's things. The clothes smelled of mothballs and Old Spice.

"Maybe finding these was a good omen," Carlos said.

"What do you mean?"

"You need something for the visitation, right?"

Henry agreed.

"Since he loved the team so much, wouldn't it be a nice tribute for him to wear it on his way out of this world?"

As soon as Carlos said those words, he knew they might be taken the wrong way.

"I didn't mean anything bad by that."

"I get what you were trying to say," said Henry.

Henry sighed, letting the emotions wash over him.

"I think it's a good idea. I think he would have liked it. Thanks, CJ."

Henry moved the box over to the far side of the bed and continued to search through the rest of the items on the ground. Carlos went back to the closet and brought out another box. This one contained a full load of baseball gloves. They were all neatly stacked on top of each other and completely new.

As he opened the box, the tinge of leather and moth balls wafted up his nose. The clear packing tape remnants on the sides showed nobody had opened the box until now.

"Wow, look, an entire box of brand-new baseball gloves. Ever play?"

Carlos removed one from the box. The tag was still dangling from the glove, placing it in his hand. As he slipped his hand in, the glove felt off to him. Granted, Carlos was no baseball player, but he played a few games in his youth to know what a glove should and shouldn't feel like. The weight of it seemed strange to him. Carlos remembered seeing a documentary during his baseball phase in middle school.

From what he recalled, the glove comprised several layers of leather, and the fingers had inner pockets that were joined tightly with the lacing and inseams. The layers gave the glove the feeling that Carlos was now lacking.

"No. I never played."

"Something feels off on these gloves. They seem lighter somehow."

"Um. Well, I wouldn't know. Those probably belonged to the Valley City PD charity team he coached. You know about that, right?"

"Yeah. I figured that much. They still feel *off*."

Carlos grabbed another, and it felt the same way, so he tried half the box, and they all had that lightweight feeling. On the last one he tried, the stitching came loose on one finger. It caused a gap wide enough Carlos could fit two fingers into it easily. Where the layers in the gloves normally were airtight, these seemed to have a gap between and wondered if these gloves were made this way intentionally or by mistake.

If it was a mistake, then the rest of them would be airtight. They weren't. With his pocketknife, he opened up several more and found the same gap in all of them.

Carlos almost forgot that Henry had been staring at him the entire time, entranced in his movements.

"Something's up with these gloves. Mind if I take a closer look?" asked Carlos.

Henry gave a quick shrug. "Sure."

Carlos continued inspecting with his pocketknife, turned the box over and read the shipping label on it. The return address, which read Wilson, was delivered to Ruben Delgado Graphics in Treasure Hills.

The feeling in his stomach returned and churned harder than before, remembering now when he had searched his shop the night before; he had found boxes of baseball supplies for the upcoming summer season. It included numerous baseball gloves. It hadn't dawned on him that for a team of fifteen, the number of gloves he found seemed overkill.

Carlos now wondered if Ruben was keeping those gloves for a reason. To be more specific, the hollowed, lighter gloves instead of regular ones and in such abundance.

"I know this is going to sound way out there, but hear me out. What if Ruben was using these gloves to hide the drugs we couldn't find when we searched his shop?"

Henry's face bore no emotion or expression. Carlos couldn't read it and didn't know if he said something truly stupid or something remarkable.

"That's a bit of a stretch, CJ, don't you think? Are you sure you're not reaching?"

Carlos knew how he sounded. He wasn't even sure if he believed himself, but there was only one way to find out.

"I've got to check it out. I'm sorry, but do you mind if we finish this up when I get back?"

"It's okay, go. I'll be here."

22

Carlos raced back to his truck and sped off out of Basin Circle and down the long, winding road toward Treasure Hills. As he left the neighbourhood, Carlos noticed a white Mercedes with its lights off. Assuming it was following him, he memorized the license plates and wrote them down on his phone for later. He didn't have time to stop. Finding Ruben took precedent.

Having broken several speeding violations, Carlos arrived at Ruben's Graphics in under minutes, bypassing the guardhouse with his badge. The parking lot was empty, and street lamps had just turned on because of the evening sky. Without a warrant, Carlos would have limited options, and he hoped Ruben would provide him with a reason, any reason, to search his place.

The business sign displayed OPEN, and Carlos carefully opened the unlocked door. He entered and identified himself as the police. There was no sign of Ruben, or anyone, for that matter. The lights were on, and the computer monitor and cash register seemed active. Even the promotional television in the corner was still playing ads for the Subway shop down the corner. Someone had left with little care.

Nothing seemed missing or stolen and as he entered the backroom, Carlos found no sign of Ruben. He found the boxes of gloves he was looking for. The only box that was not sealed up was the one on the top. He shuffled the box down and counted fifteen new gloves. These gloves felt heavier than the ones at Henry's. The weight was still off, but they were indeed heavier.

Upon closer inspection, he found someone altered the inside lining and removed the stitching. He poked his finger in, but instead of a hollow gap, his finger touched a small plastic bag. Shaking the glove, small baggies of what looked like meth fell out.

That was all he needed. He had found his proof. This time, he would do things the right way. He called for backup and waited for them to arrive so they could secure the scene. He did not know where Ruben had fled to.

After the officers arrived, he wanted to head over to Ruben's home to have a look around, but went to the south side of town near Rangerville Road, where this whole mess had begun. The area was always a hotbed of meth activity and could conceivably be home to a safe house or two. As Carlos got closer to the neighbourhood, the rumbling thunder that had been on the horizon returned and sprinkles of water hit his windshield.

When he came to a dead end on Rangerville Road and found himself in the circular government housing complex, nothing looked out of the ordinary. There were the standard fare of people hanging out on the front porch while others were clearing their lawns from a recent mowing. Carlos' presence in the neighbourhood forced most people indoors, as no one liked to see the police out and about, especially after his weapon discharge incident from days previous.

As Carlos left the area, he waved goodbye to what a thought looked like a friendly grandmother sitting down on her rocking chair, but to his surprise, the feisty lady gave him the finger as he drove away. Carlos couldn't help but chuckle. With no more ideas, he decided it would be best to go back home and see what he could find there.

On the drive over, he called the station and asked them to contact the judge on duty, Judge Romero, for a search warrant on Ruben's home and to search for the owner of the white Mercedes he had seen earlier. Carlos had dealt with Romero before and knew he could get one sooner than later. In the meantime, he could search the outside of his home.

It only took him ten minutes to arrive. Carlos could never imagine living in a place that took no less than three guardhouses to get home. He found the extremes of his privacy ill-proportioned. Carlos found the house quiet with the outside lights turned on. Pulling up, the motion sensor lights flooded his truck with a bright white light. He knocked on the front door. No one answered.

Walking around the home, a trail of lights shone as he passed certain parts of the house, making him feel like he was being followed by the white lights. Looking inside through some windows, he found the place bare and, having finally covered the circumference of the house, he came to what seemed like a large bedroom with a veranda and French doors leading in.

Through the cracks in the curtains, he saw the dresser drawers open and emptied of clothes, a lamp broken on the ground, and the hallway light flashing off and on.

Knocking on the door again and identifying himself, he tried the French doors but before he could place his hands on the knob, an orange tabby cat ran out through the crack of the door. Carlos knew the right thing was to call in for backup and report his entry, but he just couldn't let Ruben get away again.

Against his better judgement, he entered. Once inside, he could easily say the door was open and signs of struggle inside warranted his entering. It was a slim explanation at best.

The house appeared disheveled and gave the impression someone had hastily left, taking only their belongings and leaving behind everything else for the next person to deal with. Looking around, he found nothing of consequence and headed back out from the bedroom's entrance, carefully retracing his steps, leaving everything as he found it and the door ajar.

Carlos' phone's text message alert surprised him on the veranda. It was from an unknown number with a single line of text:

> You finally found me,
> Detective.
> I'm keeping your boyfriend
> company. Come, say hi. Come
> alone.

The pit in his stomach returned, and he realized he had left Henry alone for Ruben to find. He should have known. The white Mercedes, with its lights off back in Henry's neighbourhood, flooded his thoughts. Outpacing the lights around Ruben's house, he entered his truck and raced out of Treasure Hills, paying no regard to the guardhouses or speed limits. En route, he called dispatch and apprised them of the situation, but advised them to hold back until he could arrive.

Before dispatch hung up, they advised him that Ruben Delgado was the owner of the white Mercedes. The pieces were falling together finally. Henry was in trouble, and it was his fault. The weight on his chest pressed down, and he almost thought he was going to have a heart attack. He had to help.

As he left Treasure Hills and entered the rest of Valley City, the lights dimmed and caused his truck to disappear into the night until his brake lights were all to be seen speeding down Tyler Avenue.

———

By the time he arrived back at Henry's, the moon was peeking over the canals that lined Henry's house. The lights were out, and the only signs of movement were the lines of rusted red brown chachalacas that blended onto the roof. Minus the birds' hoarse squawking, all was silent. Two houses away with their lights off and waiting for Carlos were his backup. He signalled them to wait for his signal before making a move to avoid spooking Ruben. Everyone nodded and held the perimeter.

Carlos unholstered his gun and carefully walked down the front sidewalk toward the entrance. Before checking the door, he sent a text message to Captain Rankin asking him to give him a ten-minute head start before asking for his backup to move in. Carlos wasn't sure if he would approve of it or not, but that was the plan he was going on. With the phone back into his pocket and silenced, he tapped the door open.

It was dark and quiet. The ticking of the living room clock counted the seconds and almost made Carlos relax as its metronome-like precision keeping him focused. Both the kitchen and the study were empty.

He approached the back bedrooms and tried flipping the lights on, but they didn't work. Ruben must have shut the breakers off. Clicking the safety off, he entered the bedroom, gun first, to find Ruben and Henry. Henry was sitting in a restrained position in a chair, unable to move. His mouth and eyes were taped shut. Ruben stood smugly in the corner with a knife pointed at Henry. He stood there casually and waited for Carlos to make the first move.

Trying to gain his trust, Carlos placed his gun down on the ground and even separated the clip from the gun and tossed it to the side.

"Ruben, let's talk. There's no reason to do anything crazy."

Carlos held his palms open and outward toward Ruben.

"About what?"

"Whatever you want, man. For example, why are holding Henry hostage? What is the purpose of that?"

"Isn't it obvious? You have feelings for this douche."

Ruben tapped the edge of his knife on Henry's head.

"So, it was a wonderful motivator to get you to show up."

Having cut the power, there was no AC. The sweat from his brow was leaking into Ruben's eyes, causing them to twitch and spasm. He nervously shifted back and forth, then swiped his brow. Carlos noticed a stain forming in Ruben's armpit.

"You got me here. Now what? I'm unarmed. What do you want?"

Ruben's brow furrowed, and he seemed to get upset at Carlos' questioning.

"Things got out of control with your brother."

"What do you mean?"

"I had no choice. He gave me no choice."

Ruben became frantic and pointed the knife closer to Henry's neck. His eyes seemed chaotic and bloodshot. Carlos could see he was filled with conflicting emotions. The sweat beading on his sideburns supported that notion.

"It was me or him, and it couldn't be me."

"Stop. You're rambling."

"What I mean to say is that I had no choice but to get David arrested. Now that he is gone, thanks to you, I figured I would repay you the favour and take someone away from you."

Ruben motioned the knife toward Henry's neck.

"You set David up, but you're blaming *me* for arresting him? Is there something I'm not following here?"

The chair Henry sat in cracked under the weight. A slight break formed in one leg and was inching its way to the base of the seat. Henry continued to wiggle without bringing too much attention to himself. Carlos saw and did not indicate what he knew Henry was doing. He focused his attention on Ruben.

"Right, you arrested him because of the evidence I laid out for you."

"What are you saying?"

"Because of you, I can't be with David. Now it's your turn!"

Ruben threw his knife to the ground and quickly grabbed a gun hidden under his shirt, aiming it at the back of Henry's head.

Carlos was done talking. He kicked the side of the chair, forcing Henry to fall. A loud bang and blinding light filled Carlos' vision. He felt a burning sensation in his calf and knew instantly he had been shot. With what force he had left, he used his good foot and kicked Ruben in the back of his knee, causing him to fall. Carlos struggled over Ruben. Ruben got in a few punches but not before taking one last fist in the gut from Carlos.

With the wind blown out of him, he failed to get back on his feet. The front door crashed in an instant, and police officers quickly filled the house. They had most likely heard the gunshot and rushed in. With the two additional hands on the scene, Ruben was escorted out and arrested.

Carlos limped his way over to Henry, where he ripped off the tape from his eyes and mouth, not knowing what had just happened. With the tape removed, Henry, shocked, began to tear up. He pulled his hands to his mouth and audibly gasped.

"CJ, oh my god. Is that blood? Are you alright? Did you get shot? Where's that guy?"

Carlos couldn't help but smile. He had just gotten shot, saved Henry's life, and finally arrested Ruben. His grin would not go away.

"Why are you smiling like a crazy man?"

"I don't know. I'm just glad you're, okay?"

"To be honest, I have had no one genuinely care about my well-being like you just did in a long time. I had forgotten how good it felt to be cared for. Is that silly?"

Henry gently placed his hands on Carlos' face and smiled.

"No, it's not silly. I get it. Come here."

They embraced and held the hug for longer than they probably should have, given that they weren't alone. It didn't matter to Carlos.

23

OUTSIDE, THEY WALKED OUT AND FOUND RUBEN IN the back of one police car, sitting quietly. The moon, now higher in the sky just beyond the reach of the palm trees, was casting a reflection on the twin pine trees that lined Henry's front yard. The flashing blue and red lights canvassed the nearby houses. Neighbours gathered in doorways and on their front lawns, staring with curiosity. The wind had picked up as if energized by the commotion on the otherwise quiet street.

"Look, I gotta ask him a couple of questions before he leaves. Will you give me a second?"

Henry nodded.

Carlos gingerly stepped down onto the patio and onto the grass. Having been lucky that the bullet had gone through his leg, but the pain he had was still stinging just as badly. Unable to put much weight on his leg, he limped his way across the lawn. Carlos could see Henry wanting to help him, but he waved him away with stubbornness.

Carlos finally arrived at the car and opened the driver-side door. Ruben, with his head down, made no movements, so he flagged the officer down to let him know what he was doing as he limped to the door.

"I got to ask."

"What?" snapped back Ruben.

"Why all the Fair Park Slasher stuff? Why the clues on the business cards? Are you involved with the slasher?"

Ruben's face went from somberness to glee, then he turned his head toward Carlos and angled his head out the back of the car.

"To see this face, this reaction of yours."

Ruben pointed with his cuffed hands at Carlos and continued to smile and snicker.

"I just couldn't help myself. One day, I was reading a background report on you."

"A background report on me?"

"None of your business. I read it, and I found out about your sister and her unsolved murder. I went down the rabbit hole and found out all about your little Fair Park Slasher. Not a very bright name, eh?"

Carlos' face turned red, and his hands rolled into fists.

"From there, all I needed were a few clues left for you to find, and presto chango, you took the bait."

"But, why. I mean, what did you get out of it?"

"I told you."

Ruben eyeballed him up and down.

"This priceless reaction. Plus, I hoped it would distract you from your investigation."

"That obviously didn't work, now did it," scoffed Carlos.

"I still got to see you sweat. Watching you think your sister's killer had come back to finish the job was worth the effort. I loved seeing the pain and confusion in your eyes. Like I said, worth it."

"You're sick."

Carlos slammed the door in Ruben's face and called for

the driver of the car; waved him over and asked him to take Ruben to booking. The officer driving stopped short of driving off.

"Detective, do you need someone to take you over to a hospital for your leg wound?"

"Thanks, officer, I've got it handled. I'm on my way there now," Carlos said.

The officer rolled his window up and sped away. After he left, he went back to Henry, who had been sitting on a porch chair waiting for him.

"Sorry, I just had to get that off my chest."

"Feel any better?"

"Honestly, not really. I should take this as a win with Ruben in custody, but I still gotta take his statement and put it on record that he set up David and go through the security footage from his business and home. It's been a long case. I just want it to be over and get you the justice you deserve."

Henry smiled. "Do you think now that he's definitely being arrested that Ruben will be more cooperative?"

"I don't know. I still have to question him after he's booked. Let's hope he's in a better mood then."

Carlos could see that most of the police cars were thinning out, and the activity was dying down.

"So, do you need me to take you to a hotel or something? I'm sure you don't want to spend the night here after what happened?"

"Oh, I don't know. I don't want to go through all that trouble. I might just stay here."

"Don't be crazy. Let me take you somewhere, anywhere. Just name it."

"Anywhere?"

"Yes. Where do you want to go?"

"The thing is, I don't feel like being alone."

Carlos' colour disappeared from his face. His pulse quickened, and the sweat returned to his brow.

"I was thinking of maybe seeing if you would let me stay at your place for the night. I mean, I could stay on the couch. I don't want to put you out. I just would feel better if someone was in the next room."

"Oh, I see."

"Never mind, I've overstepped my bounds. Just take me to a hotel."

"Don't be silly. I don't mind. It'll be fun. We can Netflix and chill. I mean, we can watch a movie or something." Carlos pointed to his leg. "But first we need to stop at the hospital and take care of this bullet wound. I got my laptop in my car. Maybe we can watch the movie there, depending on how long they plan to keep me there?"

"Of course."

Carlos helped Henry grab a few things from inside his house and pack them in his backpack. They then locked up and walked over to his truck. Inside, Carlos stopped for a moment and looked at the photo of his little sister.

"Is that Amanda?"

"Yeah, I keep it here to remind me of her. She goes with me everywhere."

Carlos replaced the picture and started the truck. He headed towards the hospital and then eventually back to his place. Carlos still had some work left to do tomorrow with Ruben. In his heart, he knew David was innocent and tomorrow Ruben would give him the concrete evidence to prove it.

24

Carlos woke up to Mr. Hamster running in his cage. He never recalled his wheel being so loud before, but then again, it seemed louder since he spent the night on the couch. When Henry and Carlos got to his home, the previous night's visit to the hospital, which only ended up being a few hours long, they had mildly argued about who should get the bed.

Carlos insisted Henry take the bed, but they settled on sharing it, as they were both adults. Having been on pain medication for his wound, Carlos went straight to bed so the sleeping arrangements ending up not being such a big deal after all.

Besides Mr. Hamster's wheel, the other thing that woke up Carlos was the smell of bacon. Looking past the bedroom door and the empty bed and over the kitchen island, he could see Henry cooking enough food for several people. Carlos saw no one in his home cooking other than himself. It was a strange sight to him. He limped towards Henry from behind.

"Boo!"

"Jesus, I could have burned myself."

Carlos wasn't very good at small talk and usually just made observations when talking. He put the pan at the rear of the burner and turned the heat off, placing some plates on the island near the high-top chairs.

"I didn't mean to. How you are feeling today?"

"Hungry for sure, but otherwise I'm ok and yourself?"

"Couldn't sleep much, kept thinking about David. I just hope I can help him."

Henry stopped what he was doing and placed a hand on Carlos's shoulder.

"I'm sure once you have looked at it with a fresh pair of eyes, you'll help your brother."

Carlos nervously chuckled and crossed his fingers in a failed attempt at levity.

"Ok, weirdo, sit down. I'm almost done. Do you want toast, or I think I saw some English muffins over there?"

"Toast is fine. You really didn't have to go through all this for me?"

"For you? I was starving, and yes, partly for you. Thank you for letting me sleep here. I hadn't slept that well in a long time. With everything going on, it's been hard to sleep well. So, thanks."

"I'm glad you got some rest. And thanks for the breakfast. I'm sure it's going to be good."

Sitting at the island, Carlos watched Henry cook, remembering coming home from elementary school and helping his mother get dinner ready. His mother would let me chop vegetables while he would sneak pieces of cheese without her looking. Watching Henry chop chunks of mushrooms into the eggs made him smile. It was the strangest sensation for Carlos.

"There's that kooky smile again."

"Huh? Oh, it's nothing."

"Hmm. Now I know it's something. What you thinking about?"

"Watching you cook just reminded me of my mother," Carlos said.

Carlos swivelled back and forth on the chair and fiddled with his plate. The early morning sunlight glared on the white plates. Carlos could tell Henry was genuinely happy to be around him and felt safe.

"You hardly ever talk about your parents. You don't have to if you don't want to."

When the subject turned to his parents, Carlos's face twitched, and his head turned down.

"It's nothing. I never get to see cooking from this perspective. It reminded me of her, that's all."

"Well, speaking of eating, here we go."

Carlos watched Henry as he put down the plates of food. It was way more than he had expected. There were crispy fried pieces of bacon, expertly rolled omelets, and bread toasted to perfection. He had even placed butter on a dish to soften for spreading. It was all too much for Carlos to take in.

"Don't tell me you became a vegan in the last eight years, and you didn't tell me?"

"What? No. It all just looks so good. I don't know where to start."

Carlos saw Henry grinning from the other side of the island.

"Why are you laughing at me?"

"I'm not laughing. I'm smiling. There's a difference. It's just that you look so cute. You almost looked overwhelmed."

"I'm not overwhelmed. I'm just not used to being treated like this."

"Like what?"

"It's just nice, is all."

Their conversation ceased as they dug into the food. As Carlos ate, he noticed the stillness of the morning. Mr. Hamster's squeaking filled the background while the scraping of his fork and knife carved away at his food. He rarely ate this heavy in the morning, but on this day, it felt right.

Carlos knew in an hour he would come face to face with Ruben once again. He knew he couldn't fail his brother. That depended on him. Carlos wanted to show David that despite everything that had happened between them, he would be there for him.

AFTER THE FOOD HAD SETTLED, HENRY accompanied Carlos to the police station. When they arrived, he led Henry to his desk, where he asked him to wait. In the interview room, Carlos found Ruben already waiting.

Carlos looked at the file hanging on the side of the door and read Salinas was assigned to question him. He looked inside the room and couldn't see Salinas. Carlos observed Captain Rankin talking to Julio Alfaro in the other interview room. He did not know where Salinas was. To capture Rankin's attention, he tapped on the window. Hearing the noise, Rankin came out of the room.

"Alvarado. You're here, good. Have you seen Salinas?

"Um, no, I just got here. Why?"

"Doesn't matter. If you see him, just stall him. Don't let him in the next room. I'll explain in a minute. I got to finish this conversation up."

"Understood, Captain."

When Carlos checked around, he still couldn't find Salinas. It wasn't until he looked in the break room that he found him at the coffee station, picking through some donuts.

He headed in to stall him. Salinas seemed to be in no rush as he was flipping through the pastries.

"Hey, they got any sour cream donuts? Those are my fav."

Startled, Salinas spilled his coffee onto the ground. Carlos helped him with the mess, but Salinas brushed him back.

"Here you can have the last sour cream. I don't mind."

Salinas nodded and chugged his coffee down.

Carlos wasn't sure what to say to keep him talking. They weren't exactly friends and didn't work together on many cases, so he took the most direct approach.

"Wait, before you go, I wanted to ask you. What do you plan on asking, Ruben? What's your strategy?"

Salinas stopped mid drink to speak.

"Obviously, I'm beginning with the drug angle and building from there. Why are you asking? Aren't you going to observe again?"

By now, Carlos saw Salinas' face tensed up.

"Yeah, of course, but I just was kind of curious to hear your thoughts, you know?"

Carlos was not adept at stalling and didn't know how much longer he could keep Salinas from wandering off. From around the corner, Rankin flagged Carlos and waved for Salinas to come through.

"Turn around. Looks like Rankin wants you to start the questioning. Let's go."

Rankin stood with Sergeant Moody at his side, awaiting Salinas. Carlos could tell that Salinas was nervous about something. His pace toward them had slowed and cracked his knuckles and fingers.

"Hey, Captain, is Mr. Delgado ready?" asked Salinas.

"He is, but I don't need you to worry about that for now."

"Why?"

The colour on Salinas's face almost faded in that instant.

"I just had an interesting conversation with Mr. Alfaro, the other witness in the case, remember?"

Carlos watched as Salinas just barely registered a response.

"He had a story to tell us. Imagine this, he claims to have seen you at his place several times dropping off other individuals for his quasi-medical care, dropping off drugs from Mr. Delgado, and most importantly has second-hand knowledge of David Alvarado and Ruben Delgado as his place."

Everyone stood in silence and waited for Salinas to speak up. When he didn't, Carlos did.

"Are you not going to say anything to the captain?"

"I don't know what to say. Are you really going to take the word of a meth head?"

The captain's face was now flush with redness, and his brow furrowed.

"I would choose your next words carefully, Salinas. We have his and Mr. Delgado's testimony on your involvement, not to mention the cameras at Mr. Alfaro's cabin, which you have been there frequently. It's best you come clean now."

Salinas left the hallway and found a bench to sit down on. Rankin nodded Carlos over to Salinas. Carlos could see the worry across his face and found him mumbling to himself.

"Salinas, mind if I sit," asked Carlos.

"I don't care."

"Talk to me. What's going through your mind?"

"I can't believe how stupid I was."

Salinas was now head down, holding it down with his hands. Carlos looked over to Rankin and signalled he needed a minute with him. With reluctance on his face, Rankin agreed.

"If there is something you want to tell me that could help David, why don't you just come clean? I'm sure if you appear to be cooperating with us, we could show some leniency."

"You don't get it, Alvarado. I can't. If I do, jail is the least of my worries."

"What are you saying exactly?" asked Carlos.

"I will not spell it out to you. I just can't."

"Salinas, it doesn't look good for you. Rankin has all the evidence he needs. He asked me to come over here as a courtesy, so as not to make a scene. Think about my brother, please. Just admit what we already know."

Salinas stood and nodded over to Carlos and walked toward Rankin. Rankin waved him over. At the speed Salinas walked over, it made the length of the hallway seem like a football field. Instead of keeping a single track, Salinas bolted toward the back office where he was tackled by officers waiting.

"Please don't. I can't believe that fuck. Ruben gave me up. I don't know what he told you, but I got a lot on him. You are going to want to hear what I have to say."

Carlos could believe Salinas. He went from zero to a hundred in two seconds flat. Hearing Rankin had been just enough to push Salinas over the edge.

"Salinas, whatever you have to say can wait. What I need to know is, was David responsible for Mr. Morelo's death?" pleaded Carlos.

Salinas shook his head.

"No."

"Then who was it?"

"I was the one who dropped off the pills for Ruben at his post office box and helped him set up the fake email accounts we used to communicate anonymously. I have the usernames and passwords for the accounts."

Inside, Carlos wanted to scream for joy, but he had to keep his composure. He flagged Moody over and nodded to Rankin. Salinas glanced directly at Carlos.

"Alvarado, promise me you'll help me."

Carlos bowed his head slightly.

"Moody, please place Salinas under arrest and read him his rights."

Salinas went quiet. Carlos could not believe what had just happened. Salinas had given up Ruben. Now that they had him in custody, all that remained was to charge Ruben. More importantly, David would be free.

25

Carlos stood outside, holding for what seemed like forever, waiting for David to appear. Holding was unusually quiet for midday and in the distance, room two opened, and David appeared. He never saw David run in his entire life except the one time when they were kids. Their father was one of the lucky few that summer to buy a Slip n Slide. Carlos and David were sitting at their desks doing homework when their father called them outside to the front yard.

Once outside, their jaws dropped. Carlos couldn't believe that his father had set up the slide outside without no one having found out. The water had been turned on, and the slide was slick. He looked at his father, unsure of what to say. Watching, he simply ran at full speed to him and their father, giving him the biggest hug before running down the slide.

Carlos wanted to run the length of the hallway but didn't and instead waited for David to come up to him. Stopping short of Carlos, David grabbed his belongings from the discharging officer and signed himself out. Carlos received a message from Rankin confirming that Salinas would be put in front of Judge Cortez, who was known for giving people second chances. It was all Carlos could do for Salinas and only hoped the judge would be open-minded with his sentencing.

David's hug interrupted his thoughts and wished the hug they shared had lasted longer. Carlos could tell David was excited and confused at the same time. He signed out at the desk and got his belongings before meeting Carlos at the outside discharge area.

"Dude, what happened? How did you get me out?"

He was waiting a long time to give David the good news that he almost forgot what to say to him when the moment came.

"Spill it, man. I'm dying to know."

Carlos told him about how Ruben had been the mastermind behind everything that had happened to Mr. Morelo and how he had set him up to take the fall. He told him about the secret emails, the inside guy he had at the station, and he told him why Ruben did it all.

The look of amazement on David's face was a combination of stupor and astonishment. He also told David about how Ruben had given Mr. Morelo a fatal dose of methamphetamine to kill him.

Upon learning Mr. Morelo had been unnecessarily killed with meth, David's gaze fell to the ground. It was almost a look of disappointment and culpability. There was no way that David could blame himself for Mr. Morelo's death, but the look on his face told another story.

"We need to meet up with Henry. He's at my desk. Let's go grab him before I drop you off at home."

David nodded, and they walked the outside perimeter, following the sidewalk until they came to a side entrance that was secured with a keycard. Carlos barged in, and they found Henry at Carlos' desk nodding off. Carlos quietly walked up to him and, with a single finger, poked him awake. Henry's head tilted off his crossed hands and knocked against his computer monitor. He grabbed his head and looked around franticly.

"Huh."

"Sorry, I really didn't mean to wake you."

Carlos couldn't contain his grin.

"Right. Your brother is out. Does that mean?"

"Sure does. He's free."

"And my father's killer?"

"In custody. We had another witness come forward and clear David's name with solid evidence implicating Ruben. There's more to it, but suffice to say, your father's killer is behind bars."

Henry squeezed Carlos' body, crying intermixed with bursts of laughter and sniffling.

"Hey, I'm glad too that this is all over for you. You deserve something good in your life."

Carlos squeezed back, but not before forgetting David was standing by quietly, awkwardly fidgeting in response to their exchange.

"Look, why don't we get out of here? Henry, do you want to come by? We can have a drink and just decompress?"

Henry nodded. He agreed to follow Carlos and David back to their house and meet them there. The car ride over was quiet.

Carlos thought David might have been more excited to be free, but he looked somber. Carlos didn't want to interrupt his thoughts, so he drove in silence.

***

AFTER HAVING SOME SNACK MIX AND A COUPLE OF beers, Carlos finally got the will to bring up the funeral to Henry, who was avoiding the subject most of the evening.

David had already retreated to his room to take a nap, who seemed to do a little better.

The worst of the withdrawals were behind him like the shaking, nausea and sweating. He would just have to contend with a lot of sleep and getting his body use to food again. Having Henry alone provided the best chance to bring it up.

"So, I'm sorry to bring it up, but did you finalize your father's funeral arrangements? Isn't it tomorrow?"

Henry placed his beer down, and the glimmer in his smile disappeared.

"It's alright. You don't have to tiptoe. I talked to the funeral director. It's for tomorrow. The viewing is at noon, and the burial is at 2:00 p.m. You're still going to come, right?"

"Definitely. I'll be there. Is there anything I can do?"

"I need a ride back home to get some clothes and a ride to the funeral home. You think you could do that?"

Carlos nodded. Flipping through the channels, they found *Back to The Future* playing on Netflix and silently agreed to watch it. As they watched Marty juggle the situation involving his own father, it was hard for Carlos not to think about Henry and his father.

Carlos' father was still alive, albeit in another state and hardly on speaking terms. His mother served as the intermediary for most of their conversations. It wasn't the same as having a parent die. There was no proper way Carlos could know how Henry was feeling.

From the classes he took on human body language during his police academy days, he could tell that Henry was tense and in deep contemplation. Henry's forehead wrinkled, his brow furrowed, and he hunched over his back. Not only was the poor back posture probably creating physical pain, but it showed off his poor emotional state.

Carlos wanted to console Henry but was unsure of how to do it. On the screen, he watched Marty endlessly try to force his father into a situation that would cause him to be born but failed multiple times, continually unsuccessful until Marty stopped trying to force the situation just stopped and became his father's friend. He was there for him when he needed him the most. It made Carlos realize there was no "magic bullet" answer to how he could console Henry. He just needed to be there for him. He needed a friend.

As if on cue, when Marty's picture came back to life while playing guitar, Carlos placed his arm around Henry and squeezed him tight. There were no words exchanged, just a simple smile between the two. As the credits rolled and the next movie started, they covered themselves with a blanket and waited for the next day to begin and the funeral.

26

THE TV WAS TURNED OFF, AND MR. HAMSTER'S wheel, which was running at full speed awoke Carlos, and quickly remembered that they needed to stop by Henry's place before the funeral, making his anxiety set in. Glancing at the wall clock, he saw it read 8:30 a.m.; they had plenty of time to get ready. Henry fell asleep in Carlos' arms and looked peaceful as he slept. Carlos tried to dislodge himself without waking Henry, but it was impossible. He shook Henry, but he made no movement.

"Hey, sleepyhead, wake up. It's after 8:00 a.m. I need to get ready before heading to your place."

Henry's face looked rested, the lines on his forehead lessened.

"Good morning. That was the best sleep I've had in a while. Thanks. You really didn't need to stay out here with me, but I'm glad you did."

They exchanged smiles, and Carlos made his way to his bedroom to shower and get himself ready. Before entering his room, he stopped by David's and knocked on his door and opened it.

"Hey, you awake?"

Carlos realized asking such a question was stupid, given David was obviously still knocked out. Hoping to wake him, he tapped on the door several more times. Then he peeked into the room, which still had piles of clothes clean and otherwise squished under his body.

The blinds closed tight and another incense burning its last embers echoed in the room. The alarm on his phone beeped away, unknown to David. Carlos flipped the lights on the room and kicked his frameless bed.

"We've got to get ready. You're still coming to the funeral, right?"

With the word funeral, David seemed to jolt awake.

"Yeah, yeah. I'm up, I'm up. I'll shower after you. Hurry up."

It was funny to Carlos that his brother was rushing him since it was the other way around just a few seconds ago. Carlos didn't want to start another argument, so he let it go and went to shower. The water started off warm but ended cold.

As he wiped the condensation off the mirror, he could see that the dark circles had reappeared under his eyes. Carlos wondered if the stress had showed on his outside appearance. On any day, he would spend some time contemplating the day's events and planning what he would say to the people he would end up talking to that day. He treated his morning ritual as a dry run for the day. This day would be different, as he wanted to be early and on time for Henry.

After showering and getting dressed, he hurried David to do the same. They had plenty of time, but he was insistent they move as fast as they could. Only having one black suit, he put it on and gazed at himself in the mirror to adjust his tie. As he fumbled with it, he could feel something poking him from his inside pocket. After he got the tie just right, he removed what was poking him.

Carlos didn't prepare to find his sister's memorial card. He realized he didn't even bother to wash his suit since the last time his father used it, so of course his sister's memorial card would be there. He completely forgot about the card, laminated in plastic, since the funeral, and it looked practically new. Carlos didn't bother to look inside his own clothes and as he pilfered the suit now, his stomach turned and his skin flushed.

The room suddenly got quiet, and the only sound he could hear was his own heartbeat. It seemed to race then slow and repeat that pattern. It was a rollercoaster he wished he could get off.

Funerals made him feel inadequate because he hadn't been a better person for his sister, and now with Henry. As Henry sat in the living room waiting for him, he wanted to release all his nervous energy all at once, but couldn't. Carlos would have to hold his feelings back and be there for Henry and be supportive in whatever way he could.

When he opened the door to the living room, he found David and Henry talking. Carlos couldn't overhear what they had been saying. Mr. Hamster was furiously trying his best to get out of his wheel, but was getting nowhere. Carlos almost forgot to feed Mr. Hamster, leaving him an enormous pile of pellets for him to devour that should last at least until the next day.

"I guess I'm ready, guys."

Carlos turned the lights down and said goodbye to Mr. Hamster. They all piled into his truck and headed over to Henry's before making their way to Valley Memorial Funeral Home. The trip to Henry's was quick. Carlos watched Henry reemerge in a dark navy suit with a black tie. Even though it was a somber occasion, his pulse raced at seeing Henry in his suit.

Carlos hoped that if their fathers saw them now, they would be proud of them. On the drive over, the palm trees lining the Valley City Lake made Carlos think of David and their father's fishing trips. Their father was't much for taking Carlos fishing. That was something that he specifically saved for David and always made it a point to rub in that Carlos hadn't been invited. He never knew why he had never got an invitation, but it didn't matter to him.

WHEN THEY ARRIVED AT THE FUNERAL HOME, several cars had already begun filling up the spaces. Carlos rolled his truck to the front awning and let David and Henry out, and asked them to wait while he parked. The air had become humid and still with the sun peeking from the clouds, causing Carlos to sweat ragged. He heard the organ music playing in the distance that welcomed the guests. They all walked in together. Carlos eyed his brother's Air Pods in his ears.

"David, get those things out of your ear. Don't be disrespectful."

"Dude, they aren't even on. Chill."

They walked down the long hallway to the back, where the service was being held. When they arrived at the entrance, Henry hesitated at seeing his father's picture in large colour format. Santos was pictured in his Cowboys jersey, almost smirking under his thick black moustache. Carlos always found it strange people chose smiling pictures of the deceased. Carlos flagged David to go inside while he talked to Henry.

"If you need a minute, take it. There's no rush."

"I'm good. I just wasn't prepared to see my father's picture so huge; you know?"

"I totally get it."

There was a silent pause that stretched for several seconds before they moved inside. The music flooded their senses. David parked himself toward the front, where the seats were marked IMMEDIATE FAMILY. No one else had bothered to show up from Henry's family. With the casket open, Carlos froze mid aisle, confused, remembering Henry had asked for a closed casket, but perhaps he had remembered wrong.

From his vantage point, Carlos saw Santos was wearing the same Cowboys jersey and cap. Surrounding his body were dozens of roses and other flowers. In his hands were a pair of glasses and a gold bracelet. As the priest conveyed his words and prayers, Carlos found it hard not to stare at Henry the entire time. Carlos could only imagine what was running through his mind, the pain that he must be enduring. Offering a smile, he glanced at Henry again and inched his hand toward his. Their pinkies intertwined.

When it was time to visit the casket, Henry waited for everyone else to go first. The crowd had been light; only a handful had shown up. Henry didn't seem to recognize any of them, as he had spoken little during the viewing. When the building emptied, and he was left alone with his father, Carlos and David went to the back of the room and gave Henry the space he needed.

"You know, he used to come get coffee when I worked at Benny's. Bet you didn't know that, huh?" David said softly, breaking the silence between them as they sat in the back waiting for Henry.

"Really? No, I didn't. So, is that where you met him?"

"Yeah, he was a good person. The man always listened to me and never judged me unfairly. Even when he found out that I had been using, he still tried to help me. Pops was a good guy. It's such a shame."

"I know. It sounds like it. I hope Henry's going to be alright since he seemed pretty quiet during the viewing."

"Of course he was. Dude, everyone handles this shit differently. Just let him handle it his own way."

Carlos stared back at his brother and wondered where this emotionally stable person had been during their youth. Maybe all the time he spent with Santos did well. After a few more seconds, Henry walked toward them, undoubtedly ready for the burial.

After he rejoined them, they walked together back down the long hallway, where Mr. Garza was waiting for them.

"Mr. Morelo, it is good to see you again. Your father is being taken to the burial plot you chose and will be ready in thirty minutes for the service. I have one other piece of business. Your father had a will and left specific instructions for it to be read after the service with you and a Mr. David Alvarado to be present and any other guests of your choosing."

Both Henry and David seemed short on words. Carlos questioned the reason for inviting David.

"Oh, I see. Of course. Is there anything else?"

"You can meet me in my office here. The lawyer representing your father will be present to read the will."

"Thank you."

They made their way outside and found some benches to sit on as they waited for the burial to be readied. The clicking sound of the water sprinklers echoed in a regular pattern. The clouds had increased and hid the sun, if only temporarily.

THE BURIAL WAS SPARSELY ATTENDED, AND MOST OF the seats remained empty. When the priest spoke of living life to its fullest and being survived by their children, Henry openly began weeping. Carlos tried to comfort Henry by squeezing him closer and as the service continued, Carlos could see Henry began to settle. With the last words spoken by the priest and his father laid to rest, Henry said he needed a few minutes alone to say his goodbyes. In the meantime, Carlos and David retreated to the outside benches and waited for Henry.

"You know, coming here made me think of my funeral."

"What do you mean?"

"If I continued smoking that shit for any longer, it could have gone down bad, or even worse. I could have died."

Carlos looked at his brother, and for the first time, he saw his brother's sincerity and realization of his actions and how they affected not only himself but Carlos as well.

"Well—"

"I know you tried to help me, but I wouldn't let you."

"You understand now what you need to do now. Getting you healthy is all that matters. I just want to tell you that this time, I will be here for you. I won't get distracted again."

"I know. So, what do you think this will reading is all about? I mean, why was I asked to be there?"

"Your guess is as good as mine. Zero clue."

Carlos saw Henry approaching, so they stood up to meet him. They all went back inside through the doors that they exited and found Mr. Garza's office door open, and the desk emptied where he added several extra chairs to accommodate for the will reading. Inside, Carlos found who he presumed to be the lawyer waiting for them.

"Hi, I'm Detective Alvarado, this is my brother David, and this is Henry Morelo. You must be Mr.?"

"Robert Carbajal, Mr. Morelo's attorney. Are we all ready for the reading?"

They all nodded.

"Alright, please be seated, and let's get started. Mr. Morelo, your father opted out of a more traditional will and left specific instructions for how his assets would be divided and what would happen to them. Here is the list. For his life savings of thirty-five thousand dollars, he would like it to be divided in the following manner: ten thousand going to a local pet shelter and the remaining twenty-five thousand to be left to a David Alvarado for educational expenses. The funds will be placed in an educational trust under his name, with specific instructions to only be used for college or other education-related expenses. Mr. Morelo also left a gold bracelet that the funeral home has set aside for Henry."

Mr. Carbajal stopped his reading and looked up, glancing to see if Carlos' and David's attention remained. Carlos nodded slightly at him, then Mr. Carbajal continued.

"His largest asset, the deed to his house, will go to his son Henry Morelo, effective immediately. Any remaining funds from the charity donation that was set up for his funeral costs will be donated to any charity of Mr. Morelo's choosing. Last, there is a handwritten letter addressed to Henry Morelo."

Carlos stared at Henry and his brother, unsure of what to say or do after witnessing the will reading. Henry's father had been so generous to his brother, and Henry had just become a homeowner in a place where he no longer lived. He wondered what it meant for his future and what his brother would do.

Would he go to school now, given the chance, or would he continue the same path he had been on before? Carlos could only hope that his recent experience with jail would deter him from the latter.

"If there is nothing else, gentlemen, I will leave the documents here for you, Mr. Morelo, and my contact information along with the bracelet, if you have further questions. Good day and you have my condolences for your loss."

Carlos saw the lack of movement on his face overwhelmed Henry, but his eyes told a different story. They were erratically searching, as if for answers he would never find. Carlos squeezed Henry's hand, which seemed to slow the thought spiral. Their nonverbal communication was strong. Carlos could see that it had been a lot for Henry to take in.

The lawyer dumped a lot on them all at once. He just wanted to show Henry he was there for him, no matter what. Henry placed his head on Carlos' shoulder. The weight of it all just melted away, and Carlos could feel it oozing onto his shoulder. Henry closed his eyes, and Carlos squeezed harder than he had before.

"Guys, I can't believe Santos left me cash like that. I mean, we talked about school like once before. I had joked around with him I had always wanted to go to film school but like not being completely serious. I mean, it could be fun, but really, twenty-five thousand all for me. It just seems so unreal."

"It's real, David. I guess my father saw something in you. Hey, I'm just glad that toward the end, he had you to talk to. It sounded like you two meant a lot to each other," said Henry, while he grabbed the bracelet from the table and clasped it in his hand.

"Pops was a solid person, kind of the only good thing in my life, considering all the other shit that's been going on. He really looked out for me. And dude, that was sweet. He left you his gold bracelet, considering what it meant to him, huh Henry?"

"David, I'm not following you," said Henry.

"Your father told me the story behind the bracelet. Said your mom got it for him after you were born and that each little orb thing represents a single child, get it? I guess that's why he wanted you to have it."

"I don't know what to say except thank you, David. This makes his gift much more meaningful to me and I just can't thank you enough. I'm just glad he had someone toward the end that looked out for him. Everyone needs someone, and I'm glad it was you."

They stood up and gave each other one of those hugs that you only see in movies. The elongated circle hugs at the end of movies when they fade to black. Carlos sensed his relationship with his brother would get better in time, and as far as Henry went, that was a blank slate.

27

Carlos got the news Henry planned to go back to Denton at the end of the week following the funeral. He sat with the information before reacting to it and eventually figured there had to be a way to get Henry to stick around longer.

It didn't seem fair to ask someone to uproot their entire life for something that he wasn't even sure was real. Henry had school and a life back in Denton, so Carlos tried to play it cool and not message him, but after several days of no contact, he couldn't stand it any longer and broke down and texted.

> Hey, wyd?

Nothing, cleaning around here.
Why, you bored, wanna help?

> Clean? sure, when?

Lol, yes clean. now

> Ok, brt.

Carlos headed over, but before leaving his house, he peeked into David's bedroom. His brother told him he was looking into enrolling at Valley City Technical College to take some basic courses. At first, Carlos didn't believe him, but that changed when he saw him highlighting and circling classes in the student guide for classes. The feel of the room changed, with clothes piled in one corner instead of scattered everywhere. The incense was gone, and the window blinds were now open and his desk neat and organized. It was the start of something good for his brother, he hoped.

"Whatcha doing?" asked Carlos.

"Seeing what classes I want. They have Intro to Radio, Television, and Film Studies. I think I'm gonna do those to start."

Carlos stood there and said nothing back to David, who he would always see as his younger brother, who would be afraid of every little noise coming from outside their childhood room. He would always remember him as looking to him for protection. Now he would remember him as simply his brother and now a friend.

"Dude, what you staring at? You're spacing out."

"I'm not. I was just thinking."

"About?"

"Nothing. I'm glad you found classes that interest you. Hey, I'm gonna head out. Text me if you need anything."

"Where are you going?"

There was a protracted silence.

"I know where you're going. You're gonna see Henry."

Before Carlos could say anything, his smile gave it away.

"I knew it. Go for it, brother. You got it."

Carlos blushed and said goodbye to his brother. His brother was smiling as he exited his room and out the front door.

CARLOS CROSSED THE TRAIN TRACKS BACK INTO Fair Park, down Wichita and on to Basin Circle, then arrived at his house. Boxes had been collecting outside along with a PODS storage container that had been left out front. Carlos parked his truck along the side and saw Henry inside the storage container, making room for more boxes. Henry stuck his head out and waved Carlos over when he heard him honk his horn.

As he approached him, he felt dots of water on his head and hands. Looking up, he saw the clouds darken. Hints of thunder echoed in the distance. A loud clap of thunder rang across the sky, still too far away to be worried about. The dots became a drizzle, and Carlos took refuge in the container with Henry. There was no light inside except what was filtering in from the outside.

Standing next to Henry, Carlos' eyes averted his, and he slowly tapped his foot. The light tapping of the rain buzzed across the container. Carlos wasn't exactly sure what to say and knew that this might be the last time he saw Henry for some time.

The rain seemed to provide the perfect atmosphere Carlos needed for a romantic setting, but he still wasn't sure how to proceed. Carlos tried to find the right words to break the awkward pang that filled his stomach. Instead of the perfect words, he just went with it.

"Hey."

"Hey to you too," said Henry, smiling.

"Looks like you got everything packed."

"Just about."

It was excruciating how difficult Henry was making the conversation. Maybe he wasn't doing it on purpose, but Carlos needed to take the lead in the conversation. Otherwise, they would likely stay staring at each other. It wasn't obvious if Henry was just as nervous as him or simply not interested, because he started fiddling with the contents of a box.

"I know that you're leaving, and I just thought it was best to do that in person. I hadn't heard from you in days. I wanted to call or text, but I didn't want to bother you. I'm sure you have a lot of stuff to get done, and I just wasn't sure if you wanted to hear from me."

Carlos realized he was rambling and immediately stared down at his feet.

"I must sound like an idiot. I don't even know what I just said. I feel off."

Henry was closing a box up when he stopped and faced Carlos and fidgeting with his father's bracelet.

"Off?"

"Yeah, I can't really describe it. I mean, I sort of can. I just can't get the words to come out."

"If you don't know the words, then why don't you show me?"

Their eyes met, and the weight that had been holding him down faded.

"There you are. There's the smile I know."

Carlos stopped for a beat and swallowed. He slowed down enough to let himself be in the moment. The feelings that were held down by nervousness and fear suddenly came to the surface. Carlos had to take his shot, otherwise he would most certainly regret it. With his right hand, he brought Henry closer, as if he was going to whisper something close to his ear.

Instead, their lips met, making him feel like a pile of goo inside. The kiss lasted only a few seconds and when done, Carlos leaned in, pressing their foreheads together.

"I will not apologize for doing that, Henry."

"Why would you?"

"I have a bad habit of feeling guilty whenever I do anything for myself."

"Well, you don't need to do that with me anymore."
"I don't?"
"No. You don't."

TWO DAYS AFTER HENRY WENT BACK TO DENTON while at his desk at work, Carlos received an email from Henry. They spoke little since he left, other than a few casual texts. Carlos closed the rest of his browser windows and read the email:

CJ,

Sorry it took me so long to get a hold of you, but I've been busy with class. My professors let me turn in some assignments I missed with points off, but I guess that's better than a zero, right? Anyway, I finally caught up and had some time to breathe. I hope everything back home is good for you. How's work going? I'm sure it's always busy. I don't even know why I asked that. Reading it back sounds like a stupid question.

I'm rambling now, sorry. Anyway, what I wrote to tell you is that I'll be graduating this summer after all. I had a meeting with my counsellor, and if I take two classes this summer, it will make me eligible to graduate in July instead of December! I gave little thought to what I would do after graduation, but ever since leaving Valley City, I think about home more and more. I still have to deal with my dad's house and what to do with it.

Speaking of my dad, I finally read his letter, the one in his will. In it, he told me he always wished one day I would come back and see him, but he understood why I didn't. My dad apologized for how he and my mom treated me in high school. It was bizarre hearing him apologize like that. The last thing he wrote was that he hoped I would keep the house and

someday move back home. Who knows? I kind of got off track there. So yeah, looks like I'll be back in town come July, at least for a little while, anyway. I just thought you should know.
Henry

Carlos closed his email and picked up his phone to text Henry and began typing a message, but then deleted it. Before he rewrote his message, his phone beeped with a message. It was from Henry.

```
fyi, sent you an email.
oh, and hi!
```

Carlos saw the three dots where a new message was being typed. It would start, then stop, and then start again. Nothing else came through. He responded.

```
                        Hey. yeh I read it.

And?

                        And it sucks July is so far
                        away.

I know

                        I don't mind waiting.

Me neither, CJ.
```

CARLOS WAS NEVER IN SUCH A GOOD PLACE IN HIS life where his personal relationship with his brother was at an all-time high. They were talking, hanging out, and even making plans. Carlos forgot what it felt like to truly have family around him, to have a support system for when things went bad but also for when things were good to share with. Even his love life was on the up and up with Henry, although with delayed gratification since he would not be returning to Valley City for several months.

Until then, Carlos would do what he does best, finding and arresting the criminal scum of Valley City and keeping his neighbourhood safe. Ever since he got the faux pas from Ruben of the Fair Park Slasher calling card, it was festering and growing like a fungus in the back of Carlos' mind. He knew the only way to remove it was to confront it head on, which meant going full force back into the Fair Park Slasher Case. Carlos owed his sister that much.

Perhaps time would provide a fresh perspective that would prove useful. Regardless, he would never give up on his sister until he found the truth.

Author's Note

Writing this novel has been a journey that started almost 10 years ago in one form or another. The kernel of the story started as a short story about a police detective in a small town dealing with the seedy drug underworld. After I wrote that story, I never did much with it and to be honest I almost forgot about it until I started my MFA at Southern New Hampshire University (SNHU) when I began thinking about what my manuscript should be. I began looking at my old short stories and dusted them off and found that one and repurposed it to what would eventually become *A Deal Gone Wrong*.

What I want to say most about this novel is its fictional setting of Valley City. I used Valley City as a stand in for the greater Rio Grande Valley (RGV) which is in South Texas. If you are not familiar with the location, it is a four-county area on the southern most tip of Texas bordering Mexico. "Valley City" is an amalgamation of the major cities in the RGV which includes Brownsville, Harlingen, McAllen, Rio Grande City, and others.

I chose this route because it allowed me a bit more

freedom and flexibility to tell stories about my home without being restricted to the cannon of the RGV. When reading *A Deal Gone Wrong*, anyone who is familiar with the RGV will still find its essence albeit with a bit of flair.

I do want to mention that any similarities in names of characters or places are strictly coincidental. I do hope that in reading this novel you have learned something about my little corner of the world and found how unique and diverse "Valley City" can be. Until next time, keep reading and I'll keep writing.

Saul Sandoval

Acknowledgments

Along the way there were many people that were sounding boards for my ideas and very early story concepts, and I would like to express my gratitude here.

First, I would like to thank my dear friend Jose Loyola who was one of the first to read my very first short stories and give me feedback. His words and support over the years have been priceless and invaluable.

Next is Vaughn Fox but to be will always be just Jeff to me. We met back in Denton, Texas while I was doing a short stint at the University of North Texas. While there, we collaborated on some short films and screenplays. Jeff also gave me feedback on several of my short stories that would ultimately become *A Deal Gone Wrong*. I will never forget his support.

While at Southern New Hampshire University, Professor Jessica Barksdale gave me immeasurable support with my manuscript and helped me throughout it's entire process. I could not have done it without her.

I would also like to thank Vanessa Anderson of Night Owl Freelance who helped me with the early editing of my manuscript. Thank you for all your assistance.

Next, I would like to thank my partner Matias who has put up my endless hours of writing during our free time when we could have been doing other things. I thank you for understanding and supporting my dream and career.

Lastly, I would like to thank the team at Wicked Ink Publishing for taking a chance on a first-time novelist. Your continued support has meant the world to me.

About the Author

© Saul Sandoval

Saul Sandoval, rooted in the vibrant Rio Grande Valley of South Texas, is a storyteller at heart. From studying Creative Writing and English at the University of Texas Rio Grande Valley to honing his narrative skills with a master's in fine arts in Creative Writing from Southern New Hampshire University, Sandoval's journey is a testament to his commitment to storytelling. Inspired by his surroundings, he crafts narratives that shed light on the rich complexities of the Rio Grande Valley, aiming to amplify the voices and stories often overlooked.

Beyond writing, Sandoval explores mystery and science fiction and, alongside his partner, embarks on adventures both local and international. Sandoval's multifaceted approach reflects a genuine passion for storytelling, a dedication to his community, and an adventurous spirit.

instagram.com/ssand1984

x.com/ssand1984